"Scarlett, it's late."

She turned to look up at him. He stood close and her heart beat faster as she shook her head. "I can't quit."

"Yes, you can, for a little while. Come on. Let's get a couple of hours of sleep before the sun comes up. I've got a blanket in the back of the pickup."

Luke was bare-chested, too appealing, too nice, too damned handsome. His looks had gotten better over time. Her gaze drifted to his mouth, to memories of his mouth on her body.

"You remember just as much as I do," he said in a deep, husky voice that played over her like a caress.

"I may remember, but that's all. It won't go any farther than a memory," she whispered.

"Scared to kiss me, Scarlett?"

"Don't try to goad me into doing something in anger that I wouldn't do otherwise," she said, annoyed with him—and with herself. Because she wanted to wrap her arms around him and kiss him until the sun came up...

* * *

Reunited...with Baby is part of
Texas Cattleman's Club: The Impostor series—
Will the scandal of the century lead
to love for these rich ranchers?

Dear Reader,

Here is another Texas Cattleman's Club story! Tech genius Luke Weston flies in on his private jet from Silicon Valley, California, to Royal, Texas, to save his family's ranch. And to help his friend Will Sanders. Someone has been posing as Will and stealing money. Luke's company has newly developed anti-fraud software that Luke hopes will help catch the culprit. He is happy to return to Royal, but it means seeing the woman he fell in love with years ago and has never forgotten.

In the past, Scarlett was heartbroken when Luke left town. Now that he is back, neither one wants another heartache. He's a billionaire who dates celebrities and she knows he would never marry her—Scarlett is a small-town vet. Luke feels he comes from bad blood. They know they don't fit together and would be bad for each other, so they fight the fiery attraction that has never ended and sizzles with every contact...with little success.

Thank you for your interest in this book. Find me on Facebook as Sara Orwig, Romance Writer or go to my website, saraorwig.com.

Best wishes,

Sara Orwig

SARA ORWIG

———

REUNITED...WITH BABY

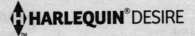
HARLEQUIN®DESIRE

Special thanks and acknowledgment are given to Sara Orwig for her contribution to the Texas Cattleman's Club: The Impostor miniseries.

Recycling programs for this product may not exist in your area.

ISBN-13: 978-1-335-97148-7

Reunited...with Baby

Copyright © 2018 by Harlequin Books S.A.

Printed in U.S.A.

Sara Orwig, from Oklahoma, loves family, friends, dogs, books, long walks, sunny beaches and palm trees. She is married to and in love with the guy she met in college. They have three children and six grandchildren. Sara's 100th published novel was a July 2016 release. With a master's degree in English, Sara has written historical romance, mainstream fiction and contemporary romance. Sara welcomes readers on Facebook or at saraorwig.com.

Visit her Author Profile page at Harlequin.com, or saraorwig.com, for more titles.

One

On a Wednesday, the first of August, Luke Weston gazed out the window of his Gulfstream jet as his pilot flew east to Royal, Texas. Looking down at the wide-open, mesquite-tree-covered landscape, it struck him that he was flying directly over the Double U. The ranch that he had grown up on and was now returning home to save.

As he stared out the window, he wondered if he should let the Texas ranch go once and for all. It was no longer home to him. Ever since graduating from Stanford six years ago, he'd been living in Silicon Valley, where he'd been working tirelessly to build his company into the tech-world juggernaut that it was today. He had no desire to live anywhere else.

Even so, he couldn't bear the thought of the

Texas family ranch being auctioned off because his drunken father had mortgaged the Double U again and then couldn't keep up with the payments. Thank heavens, he wasn't like his dad. But when he was young, his dad hadn't been a drunk—a scary fact that was impossible to forget. And his grandfather on his dad's side had been a drunk later in life, too. A drunk who was killed in a bar fight. Bad blood.

Luke's thoughts shifted to his hometown friends, especially Will Sanders. Unable to attend Will's funeral because he had been in Europe, Luke had heard about Will crashing his own funeral in Royal and all hell breaking loose. Who had been impersonating Will? That had been the big question, but answers were pointing in one direction.

This morning, before Luke left California, Will had phoned to inform him that his lifelong friend Richard Lowell had been the one passing himself off as Will. But then Rich had disappeared and no one had a clue where he was now. Another friend had also gone missing—Jason Phillips. At present, only the police and those close to Will knew about Rich, and they were still keeping it quiet while they tried to piece together all that had happened. Will had confided in Luke that Rich had tried to kill him on their annual fishing trip, pushing Will overboard and leaving him to drown. Will was rescued and survived to come home to his own funeral. The body had been cremated, so all they had left were ashes and bones to try to identify.

Adding to the mystery, Will told Luke that funds had been pilfered from the Texas Cattleman's Club in Royal and they believed Lowell was the responsible party. Upon hearing that, Luke told Will he thought he could help him find the missing imposter via the antifraud software that he and his team at his company, West-Tech, recently created that could aid in following money trails. Will had been interested in learning more, and they agreed to discuss it in person once Luke arrived in Royal.

Once again, Luke reviewed his three purposes in going back to Texas. First, he felt compelled to save the ranch that had been in his family for more than a century. He wondered in what condition he would find the family ranch. How were the animals faring, and how many cowboys still worked on the ranch? Did his dad owe them back pay?

Second, he wanted to do everything he could to help Will find Rich Lowell. The first order of business was to contact the PI who had been hired to aid in the investigation.

And the third reason for returning to Texas was that he felt duty-bound to go visit his dad in the assisted-living home where he had been residing ever since he had been diagnosed a year earlier with cirrhosis of the liver, a debilitating disease. As always, when he ticked off his plans, he had a deep awareness of another Royal resident, Scarlett McKittrick.

Scarlett was one resident he should avoid at all costs, but he suspected that wasn't going to happen. She was the best vet in Royal, Texas, so he would most likely need her professional expertise.

As he pictured her in his mind, the memories assailed him. Memories of holding a naked Scarlett in his arms, kissing her, her intense, instant response to his every caress. Luke drew a deep breath. He was *not* the man for her, and when they parted, she had been furious with him for walking out on her instead of marrying her. Even so, what he wouldn't give for one blissful night with Scarlett before he returned to his carefree, no-strings-attached existence in Silicon Valley.

But he couldn't afford to be distracted with thoughts of his ex. He had to pour all his time and attention into trying to salvage the Double U. Luke still felt a low-burning anger at his dad because he had long ago paid off the ranch and owned it outright, but Luke had made the mistake of letting his father keep everything in his name. Luke hadn't realized what was going on and that his father was pawning things off, selling livestock, mortgaging the ranch to the hilt. Luke felt partially responsible for turning a blind eye and not coming home the moment his dad had been moved to the assisted-care facility. But he'd put on a good show, and Luke had believed him when he'd said that everything was fine.

However, when Luke hadn't been able to contact anybody at the ranch, his internal alarm bells had gone off. Then he got a call from Nathan Battle, sheriff in Royal, who broke the news that he was going to have to put the ranch up for auction.

Luke told Nathan he would be there in two days to pay off the ranch and take care of all the outstanding bills. As soon as he ended the call with the sheriff, Luke had made arrangements with his pilot to fly to Texas the next day.

He just hoped and prayed he would be able to clean up the mess his father had left in his wake.

After landing in Royal, Luke called Cole Sullivan, the PI, as he'd told Will he would do, and made an appointment to talk to Cole tomorrow afternoon in Brinkly, Texas, a small town near Royal. He then phoned Will to tell him he had arrived, and the two men made arrangements to meet tomorrow before Luke met with the PI.

As soon as Luke left the airport in the new black pickup he had purchased by phone, he headed to his family ranch. As he reached the Double U and drove up the ranch road toward the house, he gazed out at the front pasture. It was worse than he had imagined. The first two horses he came across were so severely malnourished their ribs were showing, and they stood listlessly with their heads hanging down. Luke feared they would not live one more night.

He drove on to the house, passing fences that were down and a stock tank shot full of holes. Nearing the homestead, he saw a large part of the exterior wall had been ripped away, and it felt as if a knife had plunged into his gut.

Swearing harshly, he realized he'd had no concept of the full extent of the disaster at the ranch. After taking several deep breaths to help himself calm down, he placed a call to Scarlett McKittrick's veterinary clinic and felt his frustration rise yet again when he learned she was out of the office.

Luke turned his pickup around and sped toward the McKittrick place. When he crossed the cattle guard, he slowed down. As he drove up the McKittrick's ranch road, and drank in the familiar surroundings, it finally felt as if he was coming home.

Bombarded by memories, Luke gazed at the gravel road, but all that he could see were Scarlett McKittrick's thickly lashed hazel eyes. It had been a decade since he had last seen his high school sweetheart, and his life had changed beyond his wildest imaginings. Yet, no matter how much time had passed, there was no way to ever forget her.

He swore under his breath, every part of him aching with bittersweet longing for Scarlett. He had felt certain he had gotten over her, but if he had, why were memories rushing at him like floodwaters from an open dam?

A sudden wave of nostalgia crashed through him as he thought about all that had transpired between them. Back in high school, Scarlett had said she was in love with him. And for a while during his junior year, he had allowed himself to get swept up in dating her and had returned her love fully. But then, in his senior year, reality had set in.

He had a rotten background, while Scarlett had a good, solid one. Her father died when she was young and her brother, Toby, stepped up and filled in as much as he could, while Scarlett's mother quietly took over and ran the ranch with Toby's help. Luke didn't want to mess up Scarlett's life. He was afraid of the bad blood in his family showing up in him.

As his high school graduation approached, Scarlett knew he was leaving for college, but she didn't want him to go. And even though she made it clear she wanted them to have a future together, he never expected her to tell him she wanted them to marry right after he graduated. As far as he was concerned, she was too young and inexperienced to know what she wanted for the rest of her life. She could set him on fire with a kiss, but he still saw her as a kid at sixteen. She seemed far younger than his eighteen years.

He didn't want to marry for years, if ever. His parents' marriage had been unhappy all his life. At first, they fought. Later, they drank and fought. He didn't think either one had been faithful to the other. He didn't want to pass his genes on or marry someone like Scarlett and ruin her life. Only sixteen and hopelessly in love, she didn't understand. Consequently, they didn't part on good terms— something which he deeply regretted to this day.

They'd both moved on. After graduation from Stanford, Luke built his West-Tech company and he struck it rich when he invented a revolutionary—and affordable for the masses—smartphone that left his competitors in the dust.

Meanwhile, Scarlett had pursued a career in veterinary medicine. Which didn't surprise him in the least. A real softie for animals, she always tried to help any creature that needed it, loving little kids and animals as much as he loved electronics and the challenges in the tech world. As she'd been building up her vet business, she had apparently gotten engaged but was now estranged from her fiancé, Tanner Dupree, some oil heir who'd left her stranded at the altar. In Luke's eyes, no one would ever be good enough for Scarlett—definitely not himself. The oily scumbag who had deserted her didn't deserve her, either. Walking out on her on her wedding day—the guy had to be selfish and rotten to the core.

Sighing, Luke knew he was hardly one to throw stones since he'd left her, too. He still believed that was the right thing to do because, given his tainted family history, he would never be good enough for her. But honorable intentions aside, if he was being completely honest with himself, Scarlett was still by far the sexiest woman he had ever known. Even after all this time, he could get hot just thinking about her.

He had been the first guy she'd ever been with, when they were still in their teens. He remembered holding her close, her slender body melting against his. While he was here, could he entice her back into his arms for a night down memory lane…? Groaning, he quickly squelched those illicit thoughts. When he had gone to California, he'd spent too many sleepless nights in college lying awake wanting her, fantasizing about her, fighting the urge to call her because he didn't feel worthy of her because of his family background.

He didn't want to mess up Scarlett with his bad genes. He finally had put that behind him, and he didn't want to stir all those feelings up again.

It wouldn't be fair...to either of them.

With a shift of his shoulders, he forced his thoughts back to the present, determined to focus on the here and now.

As Luke approached the McKittrick house, dogs of all sizes ran toward the car. He knew they had to be strays taken in by Scarlett, and he couldn't keep from smiling while he felt a twist in his heart. He stepped out, speaking softly to the barking dogs that quieted down, the friendliest ones already wagging their tails and letting him scratch their heads.

Scarlett walked out onto the porch and stopped at the top step. His heart thudded. For an instant he couldn't speak or breathe and felt as if he was in a dream, except he knew she was real and only a few feet away. He had to curb the impulse to close the distance between them, sweep her into his arms and kiss her endlessly. She was absolutely breathtaking. When he looked into her wide, hazel eyes, he had the impact of a punch to his gut, and it was obvious she, too, drew a deep breath. As she inhaled, her blue blouse grew taut over her figure that had filled out into lush, gorgeous curves. He remembered a kid, a naive, fun young girl, but this was a woman who made his blood hot and fanned desire into flames.

While his gaze locked with hers, he lost his breath again. The urge to crush her against him was overwhelming, and he knotted his fists and focused on staying where he was. His heart pounded as his gaze swept from her head to her toes. She was wearing a blue cotton short-sleeved shirt, tight jeans and boots, and her pixie hairdo complemented her high cheekbones and big hazel eyes. Eyes that were now filled with fury.

He was dazed, stunned by the reaction she stirred in him. He had thought he was over her long ago. If he was, what was going on right now to his heart, his breathing and his lower extremities? And it was obvious from her irate expression that she also was having some kind of reaction.

Except not the kind he particularly wanted.

"You get off the McKittrick property, Luke Weston," she snapped. "And you can just go straight to hell."

"Scarlett, I need your help," he said, talking fast before she cut him off. "My dad is in an assisted-living facility and he's let the ranch go. The animals are dying and need attention—"

He knew when he mentioned the dying animals he had her. The anger left her expression, replaced by worry. She never could hide her emotions, and she was a sucker for any animal in trouble. The yard filled with dogs was proof of that.

She clamped her lips together and stared at him.

"I saw a few horses, and they look so severely malnourished that they can't even hold up their heads."

She closed her eyes for an instant as if in pain. When she opened them, he knew he had gotten through to her. "I took an oath to help animals. I'll get my instruments."

"You can ride with me, and I'll bring you back when you're through. Just save some of the horses or let's put them out of their misery. I don't know which ones to put down," he said, only half meaning it because he was certain that would convince her to help.

"You don't put any down. I'll take care of them."

"There's no feed in the vicinity. I need to get some. I'll take you with me to get supplies."

"This place is the same as it was when you lived here, and you know where to find feed and hay. Go load your pickup with whatever you need for your livestock tonight. While you do that, I'll get my things and then I'll join you," she said.

"Thanks, Scarlett. I appreciate it because I need a good vet. Those horses are in dire shape. You'll see."

Nodding, she turned away. He drove to the

barn and hurried inside. One glance at the loft and memories bombarded him. The most persistent memory was of making love with Scarlett, but he had to stop torturing himself because they had no future. He wasn't the man for Scarlett. He had done well in business, but that wasn't all there was to life. Always, he came back to thinking about his parents. His dad did well enough in business for years even after the alcohol began to cloud his judgment.

Damn, Scarlett looked good. As angry as she had looked when she first saw him, he didn't think he would have any choice except to remain cool and impersonal if he wanted her help. But that was easier said than done. He better do that for his own good. He went through hell leaving her before. Now they were adults and the stakes were higher. He didn't want to get involved and have to go through another goodbye and that's all he could hope for with her.

When they reached his family ranch, was he really going to be able to keep his hands off her?

Scarlett went inside to speak to her mother, who was bathing little Carl. For an instant worries fled as she smiled at her precious, adopted baby boy. Her heart squeezed when Carl smiled at her and held out his little arms. "I can't take him, Mom.

Luke Weston is here. He's in town and said his dad
let the ranch go and the animals are sick, maybe
dying now. He came to ask for help. Mom, I have
to help those animals."

Her mother frowned and shook her head. "I
know you're not going to ignore the livestock, so
do what you have to and then come home. You
don't need to get involved with Luke Weston again.
He broke your heart, Scarlett. Don't let him come
back and hurt you again."

"I won't. He lives in a different world now and
he'll go right back to it," she said, thinking about
the big, strapping man standing in her yard, instead of the young boy she remembered from their
high school days. He was wickedly handsome, and
her heart had pounded to such an extent that there
was no way to ignore what she felt.

As Scarlett talked to her mother, she cut up apples from a bowl her mom kept on the counter. She
bagged the apples and smiled at Carl.

Kissing her little boy's chubby cheek, she
dodged when he grabbed for her hair. She and
her mother both laughed, but she saw the worry
in her mother's eyes as she left.

Scarlett fought the urge to tell Luke she couldn't
go, but when she thought about the horses that
might be hurt or hungry, she knew she had to help.
She didn't want Luke putting any animal down un-

less it was hopelessly suffering and she couldn't save it.

She felt a tangle of emotions—shock because her pulse had raced at the sight of Luke when she had convinced herself that she was completely over him. And then there was the anger. It was always churning beneath the surface when she thought of him. Of how he'd left her behind. She didn't want to react to him or remind herself that he was more handsome than ever. He was a man now, not a boy, and so incredibly hot.

Scarlett closed her eyes and shook her head. "No, no, no," she whispered. She didn't want to find him better looking than ever, more appealing. Breathtakingly sexy. She didn't want her heartbeat to race. All of that manifested itself, leaving her gasping as if she were sixteen again, lusting like a starry-eyed schoolgirl over the most irresistible boy in Texas.

Little reminders of Luke still popped up in her life, but for all these years since he'd left Royal, she had ignored them. So she had *thought* she was totally over him, but how wrong that was. All he had to do was step out of his pickup and stride up to the porch, and she was ready to either melt into a quivering mess, or run and throw herself into his arms.

She didn't want him to come back to town and

cause that kind of reaction simply by laying eyes on him. When he looked at her, he felt something, too. She knew him well enough to know he'd had a reaction to seeing her, which just compounded her desire for him.

Could she work a few hours with him on his ranch and keep a wall around her feelings? She never wanted to suffer through another heartbreak over Luke like she had when he'd left Texas all those years ago. She had cried herself to sleep every night for more than a month.

Scarlett hurried to the closet to grab her new jeans and a shirt she liked, and then she looked down at the clothes in her hands. Whoa...what had gotten into her? Dressing better because of Luke was just asking for trouble.

"Nope, not happening," she said aloud and shoved the jeans and blouse back in the closet. She couldn't resist looking at herself in the mirror, though, and running a comb through her short hair. She guessed there weren't any women he took out in California who had freckles and pixie haircuts. She sighed because it wouldn't matter how she looked, she wasn't the woman for Luke. She wasn't risking her heart a second time because he would never make her a permanent part of his life. She had little Carl to think of now and how what she did would affect him.

Hurrying to her office, she tried to focus on what she might need at his ranch as she grabbed her bag.

Before she left she paused, pressing her forehead against the wall. "Don't let him break your heart again. Take care of the animals and then come home. Treat him as if you're with a stranger," she whispered and then shook her head as she hurried out of her room. Who was she kidding? She knew she couldn't heed her own advice, but if she could just remember he was totally off-limits and keep her guard up, she might avoid more heartache. He hadn't loved her before—now he definitely never would since he was completely out of her league. She knew he was the newest addition to *Forbes*'s billionaire list. Luke could have any woman he wanted, she was sure. In fact, she had seen his occasional picture in magazines or the news and knew he dated gorgeous celebrities and some very beautiful socialites.

Holding her bag of instruments, medications and ointments, she rushed out. Luke leaned against his pickup and was looking down at his phone. She couldn't keep from stealing a glance down the length of him, admiring his broad shoulders, his narrow waist and his long legs. When he saw her, he jammed his phone into a back pocket. He straightened and his gaze drifted slowly over her as she approached him, and all her advice to herself to pay little attention to him evaporated.

Everywhere his gaze drifted over her, she tingled. Part of her wanted to turn around and go right back to the house and lock the door. Part of her wanted to yell at him to get off their property and go straight to hell because he had hurt her badly. Yet another, more urgent, part of her just wanted to rush into Luke's arms, pull his head down and kiss him senselessly. She sucked in a breath, and her hand tightened on the handle of her bag while she struggled to think about something besides Luke, his hands and mouth and her pounding heart.

He opened the door to the truck for her, and when she came close, he reached to take the black bag from her. When his big, warm hand closed on hers, she thought her knees would buckle. It was the first time in years—since he'd left for college—that he touched her, and the slight contact sent a sizzling current racing to settle low inside her. Longing rocked her, and she had to take a deep breath and clench her fists.

"I'll put your things in back," he said, his voice raspy, which happened when he was aroused. She couldn't answer him and merely nodded. They knew each other so well. He knew she was having a reaction to being with him, and she knew he was having his own reaction to her. That made the moment hotter and more intense, and kept dredging up memories of their lovemaking when he had lived in Texas.

Again, he took her arm to help her into the pickup—help she didn't want or need. Help that made her quiver and have to fight more memories of his hands on her. When he closed the door and walked around to the driver's side, she inhaled deeply and watched him. A breeze tousled his dark blond hair over his forehead. He looked sexy, more handsome than ever—something she didn't want to acknowledge. Luke was tall, with scruffy stubble on his jaw, and he had gorgeous blue-green eyes, broad, powerful shoulders and well-shaped hands. Hands that could carry her to paradise. In short, Luke was a fantasy come to life.

He slid behind the wheel, closed the door and started the pickup, glancing at her. He sat too close, looked too enticing. "Thanks, Scarlett," he said in a husky voice that still wasn't his normal speaking voice and she knew it.

She nodded. "Let's get this over with," she said curtly, staring out the front window, fighting to ignore him as much as possible. What was happening to her? She was over him, over the hurt he caused when he left for California and said goodbye without a second thought. The old familiar anger and pain made her sit up straight and look out the window as he drove away from the house.

"Stop at the barn, and we can get some bales of hay," she said.

"I did. They're in the back of the truck. I loaded up hay and feed, and then drove back to your house to wait for you." He spared her a quick glance. "I'll reimburse you for everything. I appreciate not having to go back to town to get supplies. I'm guessing there's nothing at the ranch—just on the drive in, the place looked abandoned. There were signs of vandals, and the animals have been left to die," he said gruffly. "I was just there a few minutes, but it's clear I have a catastrophe on my hands. I want to save what animals we can."

Scarlett knew Luke so well that she could tell he was angry with his father. When they drove past the barn on her family ranch, she stared ahead, sitting stiffly, fighting yet another wave of memories.

"You still have the big barn," he rasped.

"We're not going down memory lane," she snapped without looking at him. But she was already down it. Her fingers knotted and she fought the urge to glance again at the barn she saw every day of her life, yet it held special memories of an unforgettable night.

Her whole family had been away for a barn dance. Early in the evening, Luke had coaxed her to leave with him. They had gone back to her place because everyone had gone to the party. Instead of driving to the house, Luke had stopped at the barn. The minute they stepped inside, he pulled her into his arms to kiss her. Later, he spread a blanket on the hayloft and drew her to him again to make love to her, her first time.

Looking away from the barn, she tried to think of something else and forget that night so long ago, forget memories of his slow, sweet kisses that made her want him with her whole being, memories of his strong arms around her, his mouth on her, his seductive hands all over her body.

"How are your mom, and Toby and his wife?"

"They're fine," she answered, glancing at him. "Toby and Naomi have a little girl, Ava." While Luke watched the road, her gaze swept over him, once again taking in the short stubble that covered his jaw, his tousled, dark blond hair that she could remember running her fingers through too many times to count. His shoulders were broader now, thicker. Desire rocked her and she took a deep breath. Realizing once again where her thoughts were going, she turned swiftly to stare out the window, not really seeing the landmarks they passed, but remembering being held in his arms, her head back against his shoulder.

She gave a tiny shake and struggled to get her

attention off of her ex. He would leave as suddenly as he had come, and she didn't want one tiny bit more hurt in her life because of Luke Weston, especially now that she had a son to care for.

She looked at familiar land, places she had grown up, and in seconds Luke dominated her thoughts yet again.

She had to resist his appeal. In no time he would be back in his private plane, headed to California, back to his ritzy life, back to glamorous models, celebs and rich socialites, eventually marrying one who could give him the children he'd want.

"You've done well in California. You did the right thing to move out there. It suits you as much as all this suits me," she said, knowing the Silicon Valley world was his world.

"I guess you're right, Scarlett. It's my real home," he said without looking at her. He sounded casual, but his hand was tight on the steering wheel, so obviously he felt something, too. "Common sense says to sell the ranch and forget it. I won't live in Texas again. But…I can't sell it. I just can't let the family place go. It's been in our family since the 1800s." He blew out a frustrated breath. "I paid the house off three years ago, and damned if he didn't go out and mortgage it to the hilt again. He hasn't kept up his payments—no

surprise there. He's let the help go. I just found
that out before I came."

"Sorry, Luke," she said, again without looking
at him. How polite and cool they were being with
each other. "So you're going to keep the ranch,
even though you'll go back to California? You
think you'll come back to the ranch someday?"
she asked, watching him and curious about his
answer even though she knew she shouldn't care
at all. They would never again mean anything to
each other. Unfortunately, the jump in her pulse
today showed she still had to work at getting him
out of her system.

"No, I never will, but at this point in my life,
I just don't want to let it go. I know that doesn't
make sense, because California is absolutely my
forever home."

"You don't need to be in a hurry. Your dad is
still around. It may mean something to him."

"Booze is the only thing that means anything
to him," Luke said, and she heard the anger and
bitterness in his reply. "He'll never be able to live
alone again."

After they left the McKittrick ranch, they rode
quietly. Her thoughts were in turmoil because
she couldn't lose that intense awareness she had
of Luke. She never had been able to ignore him,
and she definitely couldn't now. Why couldn't she

ever see him as just another guy? She had to get over him or get hurt again. She could never be the woman for him because of her fertility problems. One man who loved her enough to ask her to marry him had already walked out on her. Luke hadn't been interested when he had never been out of Texas and was getting ready to leave the family ranch. Now, he wouldn't have any permanent interest in a small-town female vet who couldn't bear his children. If she got involved with him, he would love her and leave her and in doing that he would get to know her baby. If she let Luke in her life again, when he said goodbye, he would not only break her heart again, he would break little Carl's heart. That could be a lifetime hurt for her and her baby.

Scarlett tried to avoid remembering Luke's kisses, but whenever she glanced at his handsome profile or his sexy mouth, the memory was vivid, tantalizing, still painful after all this time. She looked at his big, masculine hands on the steering wheel, but shifted her attention swiftly because she could remember those hands on her body, working their magic. An undercurrent of longing taunted her.

She released a quavering breath. Why did her heart race when he had merely brushed her fingers with his? She remembered how much she'd hurt when he left when she was sixteen. She didn't want a bigger hurt now.

She couldn't understand her own reactions to him. She wasn't in love with him—she barely liked him because of the bitter fight before he left for California. How could he set her pulse pounding just by reappearing? She had to get over him. She didn't want to spend years longing for a guy she knew as a boy in high school. A guy who didn't want her.

They rode in silence until he turned and headed up the road toward the house where he had spent his boyhood.

The first sign of neglect was a rusty pickup smashed against a tree. She saw bullet holes where kids had probably placed bottles on it or just shot out the windows and used the truck for a target. The wheels were gone. Weeds grew up in the road that was barely visible in spots.

"Evidently, after Dad let the hands go, he sold some of the horses to subsidize his alcohol addiction." Luke scowled. "I used to send money home, but he just bought liquor with it, so I stopped. I'll get a crew out here as fast as I can, but right now I wanted you to see if we can't save some of these horses. But honestly? I don't know how the horses I saw can last through the night. No one works here. The damn ranch is deserted—the animals left to starve and die."

She could hear the anger and pain in his voice and couldn't blame him for his reaction. She was equally shocked by the terrible conditions.

In minutes, Luke approached a pasture with half a dozen horses standing near a stock tank that needed water. The windmill had broken boards and wasn't working. She gasped. "Oh, no," she whispered without knowing she had spoken when she saw the horses with ribs painfully revealed and two with their heads hanging. All the horses looked severely malnourished. The stock tank had holes in the side.

"Sorry to pull you into this because I know it'll tear you up, but I need your help here," Luke said.

"Oh, my heavens. Look at the horses," she lamented. "It breaks my heart. You know I'll help these animals," she said, horrified to look at the condition of the horses. She felt sympathy for Luke, even though she didn't want to get caught up in his problems. But what he had come home to was ghastly, and he had tried to help his dad to keep the ranch in good shape.

She could certainly understand his anger and disappointment, and gave a silent prayer of thanks for her own family. They helped each other and did the best they could and always could be counted on. "Oh, Luke, this is unbelievable. I had no idea this ranch had just been abandoned. We're neighbors. Our ranch adjoins yours, and nobody in the area has said a word about it. Why didn't someone speak up? The last hands that left here—why didn't one of them contact you? How could your dad neglect everything so badly?"

"Because he's a sick old drunk who doesn't care about anybody or anything except his next drink," Luke bit out, and she was sorry for saying anything because Luke was obviously suffering over finding his home in shambles.

"I'll get the pasture gate," Luke said, getting out to drag open a sagging, battered gate made with barbed wire. He returned to drive the pickup in and close the gate.

"Sorry, Luke," she said stiffly when he was behind the wheel again. She spoke without looking at him, trying to avoid thinking about what he was going through. "We'll start. Let's get to work."

"I'll patch those holes enough to get water in that tank so they can drink. I sent Dad money to get fiberglass tanks and look what we've got—the old corrugated metal the cows have pushed against and bent years ago. Damn, I wasn't sure what I'd find here, but I didn't expect it to be this bad. Every dime I sent home must have gone for booze."

She looked around and saw three horse carcasses. The live horses had moved away from them and they were decomposing, probably torn by predators and birds.

"You have dead animals."

He sighed. "Damn. I can get a temporary crew out here to help." He parked near the horses and a few watched them while two slowly moved toward them. Luke was already on his phone, calling someone who worked for him to start trying to hire a crew of cowboys to do temp work.

When she approached the horses, her sympathy shifted to the animals, and she could hardly blame Luke for being so upset at his father for letting this happen. When Luke was a kid, the Double U had been a fine ranch. His dad was a good rancher, and he knew what he was doing to his livestock when he neglected them. At least he had to have known when he was sober. She spoke softly and got her bag of apples, but the horses couldn't raise their heads. She knelt to open her bag and get a needle to give shots that would help more than anything else.

"I'll get these horses to the pasture by the barn. There's water there. I'll get halters on them and lead them back, and you drive the pickup. You can follow the road here to the house," he said. "If there are any horses we can't move, we'll try to take care of them here."

It was almost an hour later when they climbed back into his pickup and drove toward the house.

"I came home every year for the first three years while I was in college, and it was never like this. Things were messy at the house, but otherwise, he kept things in relatively good shape." He scrubbed a hand over his jaw. "We had some good hands and a good foreman. I never stayed more than a night or two, so he must have pulled himself together.

"Several years ago at Christmas, I sent a plane for him and brought him to California. He said everything here was fine. He couldn't wait to get back here and cut short his stay. Gradually, we've grown more apart than ever, and I haven't been home. If I did make contact with him, he always said everything was going okay." Luke worked his jaw back and forth. "I should have kept up with him better and maybe I could have prevented some of this. I could have hired someone to come out here and run the ranch."

"You didn't know."

"I *should've* known. He always could carry on a decent conversation when he was dead drunk. I should have guessed what was going on."

"Luke, I'm sorry. This is a disaster."

"We'll just have to hunt for the animals. I doubt if there are any cattle left. I'm sure they've all been stolen. The horses probably were passed over at first for cattle. By the time anyone turned attention to the horses, they may have been in such bad shape no one wanted them. I just barely glanced at the house, but I'll walk through in case there are any animals in it."

Scarlett cringed when the house came into view. One wall was shattered, as if someone had tried to drive through it. Windows were smashed. Steps to the porch had collapsed. The front door was missing. Bullet holes dotted the walls, and boards had been ripped from the porch floor. Someone had thrown black paint at the house, and a big splash of paint had spilled down a wall. A living room chair was upside down in the yard, one leg broken, another leg missing.

"Oh, my heavens, Luke..." she commiserated softly. Certainly it gutted him to look at his childhood home so badly damaged.

"While neglect did a lot to the house and barn and outbuildings, vandals and thieves caused the rest," he said grimly. "My dad, because of his damned drinking, has just let our home—a damn fine ranch—go to hell."

Knowing how she would feel if it had been her home, she ached for him. "I'm sorry, Luke. How awful for you to come home to this." Impulsively, she squeezed his wrist and Luke turned, his blue-green eyes intent on her, causing a chemical re-action. The minute she touched him, the moment changed. Sympathy vanished, replaced by sizzling desire. But she didn't want to be swept off her feet by him again. She'd been through too much heart-ache because of Luke to go through more.

When his gaze locked with hers, she drew a deep breath, conscious of Luke and nothing else. Worse, she was absolutely certain he felt some-thing, too.

"I'm sorry for you, and I'm sorry for your dad. Have you seen him yet?" she asked, her words tumbling out too fast as she tried to get back to anything less intimate. But that slight touch of his wrist brought a truckload of memories pouring over her, and she felt her anger with Luke lose a bit of its intensity.

She felt sympathy for him. It would be devastat-ing if she came home to find the McKittrick ranch in ruin. She tried to pay attention to what he was saying about seeing his dad.

"No, that's on my list of things to do while I'm here. What he's done—or more accurately, *not* done—is going to make seeing him again even more difficult than I expected. He must be in ter-rible shape to let all this happen."

"Well, let's look for the horses or whatever livestock that's still here," she said, struggling to get back to business.

He nodded. "I stopped here briefly before coming to get you. I want the house torn down. I can't stand to see it in ruin. The memories from there weren't all that great anyway," he said, and her heart lurched at the bitterness in his voice. She curbed the impulse to reach out and squeeze his wrist again. It was obvious he hurt badly.

"There's a half bath in the barn, so at least we have a little in the way of facilities for us. There may be running water and electricity in the bathrooms in the house. Right now, however, we better find what animals we can while it's daylight. I'll try to get them back to the pasture by the barn, where you can do what you have to do and I can feed and water them. Can you stay longer?" he asked.

"Yes, I'll stay. I want to save as many horses as I can," she said.

"We'll take the pickup now. Later, I'll probably have to search on horseback because there are places on the ranch where I can't drive. I may have to go buy a horse because none of these can carry me on its back." He released a breath. "But for now, I've got rope in the back of the truck, some feed and a saddle if I need it, all sorts of supplies."

"All right," he said, "let's get started." He turned

his truck and as he drove she looked for any livestock. They hadn't driven a half mile when she gasped. "Luke, stop. There's an animal. It's a dog, and it's dead. I think it looks like it might be Mutt." With a pang, she remembered the dog that followed Luke around when he was home.

They got out of the pickup and walked closer. Luke knelt and ran his hand over the dog's head. "Oh, dammit to hell. That's Mutt. He was old and weak, and I guess coyotes got him."

She knelt to look over the carcass more closely, and she hurt even more for Luke because this was the ranch dog that he claimed as his.

"I left him here when I went to California because the ranch was up and running and in good shape," he said, his voice raspy with regret.

"The ranch was in good shape because you were here," she said quietly, still looking at the dog.

"The guys liked him and he was happy here. I thought he'd be better off. He looks starved. He was old and weak, but something's really torn him up."

"Luke, he's been shot. Someone shot him, and they may have done it because he was old and he may have been sick. There's one shot and it's a killing shot, so this wasn't random or someone being mean. I think he was torn up by buzzards and coyotes after he was shot."

Luke leaned closer to look as she pointed to the wound. "I hope he didn't suffer. I loved the old mutt. He was a good dog." He released a shaky breath. "I'm going to bury him. I have a shovel, and I'll wrap him in a tarp and bury him back at the house."

She heard the catch in Luke's voice, and a lump rose to her own throat. They both stood, and she looked up at him. Without thinking about it, she touched his wrist again. "I'm sorry. I know you loved him." The minute her hand rested on his, she knew she shouldn't have touched him, even though it was obvious he was hurting badly. His wrist was twice the size of hers, warm, his wrist bone hard. Something flickered in the depths of his eyes, and he gazed at her intently.

"I haven't loved much in my life, but I loved him," he said roughly, his voice grating and a muscle working in his jaw. She couldn't get her breath, and she couldn't understand the intensity of his gaze or his remark that he hadn't loved much in his life. Was he just talking about a dog—or was there more to his statement?

She wanted his arms around her so badly it frightened her, and she stepped away quickly, going back to the truck. "Tell me if I can help," she called over her shoulder.

She was breathing hard as he walked to the back

of his pickup. Pulling work gloves from his pocket, he got a tarp to wrap the dog. In minutes, he slid behind the steering wheel and drove on in silence.

Why did it feel as if Luke had been away only days instead of years? Those empty years had vanished in too many ways. The worst part was the realization that she had never really gotten over him, something she had struggled desperately to do.

She had never felt this way for Tanner, and she had been engaged to him. Was it because Luke had been the first love in her life? Or did it go deeper than that?

They rode together in silence, only a couple of feet of space separating them in the pickup, but there was still a permanent, deep chasm dividing them.

He hadn't loved her and he never would, so why couldn't she forget him? She clearly meant nothing to him—that alone should stop the volatile reaction she had to him and the desire that still steadily simmered through her veins.

They bounced over the rough ground, and she looked around carefully, trying to see any sign of livestock. In another twenty minutes she spotted horses to the east. "Luke, over there."

"Yeah, I see. They're in a fenced pasture, so let's keep looking and see if we can find some more and get them back with these. They may be in bad shape, but hopefully we can get them to the barn." He continued to drive, and she gazed around, looking for any more signs of life.

"Luke, I see horses through the trees," she said a few minutes later, and he swung the pickup in the direction she pointed.

For the next six hours they worked—rounding up horses, finding a few cattle, getting them back to the barn—trying to do it all while it was still daylight. When the horses were finally in the corral by the barn, the cattle in a pasture, Luke closed the corral gate and turned to her.

"You start checking the horses while I get feed to them. They've got water now in that tank. Shortly, it'll be dark, so I'll get lanterns out now and have them ready, and we can keep working if you can stay. If not, I'll take you home. I'd appreciate your help if you can."

"I can stay."

He looked at her and reached out to hug her. "Thanks, Scarlett," he said.

As his arms wrapped around her and pulled her against his solid, hard body, her heart thudded. His strong embrace made her tremble and want to wrap her arms around him and hold him tightly against her heart. How was she going to work with him into the night without stirring all those old feelings she had for him?

Two

He released her abruptly. "I better get busy," he said. His words were casual and indifferent. His voice was that hoarse tone he had when he was aroused, so she knew he felt something, too—knowledge which made her heart beat faster. What did Luke feel now? She shouldn't care or even think about what he was feeling.

Why, oh, why, couldn't she get Luke out of her system? When he left Texas, he had hurt her terribly, and she shouldn't feel any kind of desire for him, but she did. How could she ever trust him again? She had to guard her heart and not let sympathy for his problems make her forget their past.

"Luke, I have to call home and then I'll get busy," she said, walking away from him.

She talked briefly with her mother, making certain all was well with Carl. While Carl was fine, her mother had warnings about Luke and how he had broken her heart before. The brief conversation just reminded her again how much Luke had hurt her before and made her conscious that she hadn't gotten over him at all. She had been fooling herself all these years—easy to do when he was in Silicon Valley and she was in Royal.

It was a hot August night in Texas. Luke had lanterns going, and she looked around once just as he yanked his shirt off and tossed it aside. Her mouth went dry and her heartbeat sped up as she looked at his muscles, highlighted by the lamplight. A sheen of sweat glistened on his bulging biceps while he scooped up more hay with a pitchfork. She could remember being in his arms, held tightly against his body. Longing shook her to the core, and she couldn't stop looking at him while memories sparked more flames inside her. Only now this was a grown man with a man's broad shoulders, a man's muscled chest, a still flat, narrow waist and a hard, rippled stomach that disappeared below his belt.

He looked up, catching her staring at him. She boldly met his gaze, wondering if he could guess her thoughts and feelings. After several long, tension-fraught moments, she finally turned away. Heat burned in her cheeks. She didn't want him to see how easily he could captivate her attention, yet it was evident he knew the effect he had on her, just as she knew when she affected him.

Five minutes later she found her eyes drawn to him once again. She couldn't resist watching him when she thought he wasn't aware of it. He must work out in Silicon Valley because he was all muscle, his back and arms shiny with sweat. He'd rolled and tied a bandanna around his forehead to keep sweat out of his eyes as he worked. In the light of the lanterns, he looked incredibly male, appealing and sexy. He also looked fit and strong.

She couldn't stop glancing at him, desire making her heart pound. She tried to focus on the horses, working hard and fast, and shut Luke out of her mind and stop gawking at him.

Suddenly one of the horses collapsed, and she raced to it, kneeling and giving it a shot as quickly as she could.

It was breathing hard, making gasping noises with each breath. It was bleeding from gashes on its belly and neck.

"Scarlett, I'm going to put him down. You're fighting a losing battle. Go on to the next one."

Startled, she glanced up to see Luke standing with a pistol in hand. A cold chill ran down her spine. Instantly on her feet, she faced him as she placed her hands on her hips.

"No, you're not! I can save him. Put that pistol, away, Luke Weston, and don't get it out again around the horses unless I ask you to."

He blinked and then pressed his lips together. She didn't know whether he was biting back a laugh or was angry at her for telling him what to do with his own horse.

She was earnest, and there was no way she was going to let him shoot his livestock. "This horse will be on its feet tomorrow." She ground out the words. "I've given him a shot that will help. Give him time. Don't you put any animal down without my permission, you hear me?"

"I won't, Scarlett, but look at him. He doesn't have the strength to stand. He's all bones and he can't breathe."

"He can breathe, and I'm going to take care of him. He'll be on his feet when morning comes. I know what I'm doing, Luke, so you go back to work and leave this horse to me." She glared at him and met his unfathomable gaze. Without a word, he tucked the pistol in the back of his waistband and stalked away.

She watched him go for a few seconds and then turned her attention to the horse and forgot Luke for the next hour. She paused briefly once for another call to her mother to check about Carl and once again, he was fine and all was well at home.

She went from one horse to another, trying to tend to each one, and she thought of the carcasses they had found, of horses that hadn't survived. During the afternoon Luke had grown silent, and she knew he was furious with his dad and his fury grew with each dead animal they found. She knew he was still devastated over the dog because, as a kid, he had loved that dog.

Occasionally, as she moved around, she saw Luke working, repairing the corral fence. There were so many places where the fence was down or damaged that she hoped he could get it fixed before some of the horses wandered away. The feed he had put out held the attention of those that were able to stand to eat or drink.

Luke had rounded up some cattle, less than a dozen head. She thought of the big herds they'd had when Luke was in high school. She heard a twig snap and looked around to see him approaching again.

"Unless you've changed a lot, I know you love hamburgers more than steaks. I'm having dinner brought out here."

She tilted her head to look up at him. "How on earth did you get dinner delivered to this ranch? There isn't a café for twenty miles."

He grinned and shrugged. "My money's good for some things. I should've asked you who to call, but I remember Rusty's. They're still in business. We'll take a break and eat. Okay?"

She smiled. "Okay. If I'd known you were going to do that, I would have asked you to get more apples for the horses."

"If we're still here, I'll try at breakfast. A couple of the horses are back on their feet already. You're a miracle worker, Scarlett, and I can't tell you how grateful I am that you're helping. I'd hate like hell to have to put all these horses down. That would be about my last straw."

"You're not going to have to put any down, so forget that. I don't care how bad they are, we're going to save them, but if you'd come much later—"

"I already lost some before I got here," he said, frowning as he glanced at the horses. "I better get back to work." He turned to leave. "I'll call you when dinner arrives."

She barely heard him because she had already turned back to a gash she was stitching. The smaller white horse stood patiently, but she wondered if it would collapse any minute. It didn't seem to care what she did or that she was even there.

By midnight there were still horses that needed tending to, and Luke was still fixing a stock tank. She wanted to keep working but, mindful of little

Carl and her mother, she walked into the shadows, trying to get out of Luke's earshot before calling home.

As expected, her mother began to argue for her to come home, reminding her again that being with Luke was going to dredge up all kinds of pain.

"Do you really want to go through all that again?" her mother asked.

"Mom, I'm taking care of very sick horses and some of the cattle need attention. They're in dire shape, and I'm not abandoning them to die when I can save most of them."

"My heavens! How awful. I haven't heard anything bad like that about the Double U. Even so, Scarlett, I'm worried about you."

"Mom, this is my job, to save animals. This is why I became a vet. I'm needed here and we can already see a difference in some horses."

"Scarlett, Luke is going to hurt you again. Maybe even worse this time because you're not kids anymore. Please get out of there and come home. Baby Carl and all the family need you. You don't want to go through all that loss and hurt again, and that's what will happen if you stay."

"No, I won't. I won't let it happen." There was a long pause, and she knew her mother was giving up and could not continue arguing.

"Take care of yourself, then. We love you," her

mom said. "And before you start to get caught up in old feelings with that man, just remember that Luke will go home to Silicon Valley in a few days and you won't hear from him until the next time he pays a visit here."

She sighed. "I love you, Mom, and I love my family. Luke's dad has done a terrible thing, and bearing witness to it makes me so thankful for all of you. I'll take care of myself, I promise," she said, wondering if she really could keep that promise, or if she would just cave if Luke wanted to hug or kiss her. She almost laughed aloud as she ended her call. Her amusement fled when she looked back and saw the lights, the weak horses, the cows in another pasture. Was she being foolish and risking her heart to try to save horses that might not survive no matter what she did?

But she felt she had to stay. She had taken an oath to help animals, and she took that oath seriously.

She just hoped she could resist Luke, but then again, she might not have any reason to worry about resisting him. He probably had a woman waiting in Silicon Valley for his return.

Her attention was taken again by the ailing horses. She suspected Luke was right about the cattle. There were few left that he had found, and she imagined nearly all the Double U cattle had been rustled long ago. Luke said he would continue searching for more when daylight came, but so far he hadn't found any. She continued to nurse the horses, wondering if she would have to work through daybreak. Dinner had given her another spurt of energy, but that was beginning to fade. She glanced at Luke as he repaired holes in the water tank, going over them a second time.

He was the golden boy from Royal who had gone west and made a fortune in Silicon Valley. He hadn't been interested enough in her in high school to want to continue their relationship, to want her with him or to want to return to Royal to be with her. How many times did she have to remind herself that he really had no lasting interest in her? He had liked to kiss and make love, but he could turn around, walk out the door and forget all about her without a moment's regret. Walking out on her didn't make her blood run cold, but thinking Luke would do that to Carl did. She couldn't bear that kind of hurt. She glanced at him again. Flickering lantern lights spilled over him, turning his skin golden and highlighting his firm, muscular back and chest, his powerful shoulders and biceps, his flat stomach. She tingled as her gaze ran over him. Her mouth had gone dry, and her heart thumped swiftly. She wanted his arms around her, his mouth on hers. She could remember his kisses. Absolutely. Too well, she could recall his mouth on hers, making her quiver with eagerness, with steaming lust, with hunger for his hands and his body.

He turned to look at her. Startled, she realized how she stared as his gaze narrowed. She spun away and bent over a horse to cleanse and patch a wound while her cheeks burned with embarrassment.

She lost track of time until she glanced at her watch and saw it was after two a.m. About ten minutes later, Luke appeared and caught her wrist, lifting it as she was about to give a horse a shot.

"I think you should call it a night."

"Luke, there are still horses here I haven't treated. I don't want to stop."

"Aren't you tired?"

"Yes, but I can keep going and I want to."

He studied her and nodded. "Okay, a little while longer."

When he turned and left, she went back to work. The next time he appeared, he placed his hand on her shoulder. "Scarlett, it's late," he said. His voice was husky, his hand lightly squeezing her shoulder.

She turned to look up at him. He stood close, and her heart beat faster as she shook her head. "I can't quit."

"Yes, you can, for a little while. Come on. Let's

get a couple of hours of sleep before the sun comes up. I've got a blanket in the back of the pickup."

Luke was bare chested, too appealing, too sexy, too damned handsome. His looks had only gotten better over time. Her gaze drifted to his mouth, to scorching-hot memories of his mouth on her body.

"You remember just as much as I do," he said in a deep, husky voice that played over her like a caress.

She drew a breath and met his gaze, her cheeks burning. "I may remember, but that's all. It won't go any further than that," she whispered.

"Scared to kiss me, Scarlett? After all this time, it won't mean anything."

"Don't try to goad me into doing something in anger that I wouldn't do otherwise," she said, annoyed with him, and with herself, because she wanted to wrap her arms around him and kiss him until he would wish he hadn't pushed her into it. But she knew better than to do that.

"Okay, Scarlett, go back to work. So will I. I'll come back in half an hour or so. If you want to quit before then, just let me know."

"Of course I will," she said sweetly, running her hands lightly over a horse, feeling its bones and wondering how it could even stand. She forgot about Luke as she went back to work. She finally began to feel tired, but she still didn't want to stop.

As she worked, Luke appeared again. He reached out, and his hand closed on her wrist. "C'mon. Let's get a little sleep. The sun will be over the horizon in a couple of hours. We'll get back to this when the sun comes up."

Nodding, she didn't argue. She left him, hurrying to the barn and the tiny room with minimal facilities. Even so, she felt refreshed when she stepped out. She was so tired it shouldn't matter if they both slept in the back of his pickup, except she knew it would.

"Luke, we can't both sleep in the back of your pickup."

"Why the hell not? There's nowhere else—all of West Texas has rattlers, so the ground is out. The front seat isn't big enough. You can keep your hands to yourself, and so can I. Don't tell me you find me that irresistible?"

She knew the last part was said in jest, but she was tired and frustrated because she didn't want to end up handing him her heart again, and, if they made love, she was afraid that was exactly what would happen.

Annoyed, she stepped close to stab his chest with her forefinger. "You know you're attractive. You know I feel something, and I know you feel something, too. If we get in the back of your pickup, we won't sleep. I'm realistic enough to know that and honest enough to admit it. I can sleep inside on the front seat, and that's where I'll be. The sun will wake me."

"You sleep where you want, but after that little speech you just made, there's no way in hell I can resist," he growled, drawing her into his arms and leaning down, looking directly into her eyes. Her heart thudded. He intended to kiss her and she couldn't resist him, either. Especially when he was holding her in his arms and his mouth was only inches away, his blue-green eyes glimmering with raw, unsuppressed desire.

"Luke," she whispered, wanting him, knowing she was crossing a line she would regret, yet still unable to say no to him. The look in his eyes made it crystal clear that he, too, wanted her with all his being. Then his mouth was on hers, opening hers, and his tongue slipped inside, going deep, stroking and making her tremble, sending lightning streaking through her.

Desire shook her, and she wrapped her arms around his neck, pressing against him and kissing him in return, pouring all the pent-up longing and aching need that she felt for him into that kiss. She wanted him to remember kissing her, to want her the way she had wanted him. She hoped her kiss haunted him, caused him to lie awake at night to deal with the desire and the memories.

And she wanted to relish this moment in his arms, being kissed by him, a dream fulfilled if only for a few precious minutes. His erection pressed against her, urgent, hard, ready, and she wanted him with all her being. But then she remembered her tears, her heartbreak, her longing—he had walked away without a qualm. She wasn't going back to that.

She tore her mouth from his and then stepped away. "I'll be up with the sun," she whispered and turned to climb into the front seat of his pickup, lock the door and lean back against the seat.

She fought the urge to turn to see what he was doing. She fought an even greater urge to go back and join him, but she wasn't climbing into the back of his pickup this first night he was in town and sleeping with him. Scarlett released a shuddering breath. Was she ever going to really get over him? She thought she had—she told herself she had when Tanner Dupree entered her life, but after Luke's mind-blowing kiss tonight, she knew that Tanner had never held the appeal that Luke did.

It didn't matter. She wasn't the woman for Tanner. She wasn't the woman for Luke. Once again, she faced the fact that Luke was a billionaire businessman now, young, successful and handsome. He would not want to tie his life to a small-town vet.

Deep inside she hurt, but she also felt resigned.

She had faced reality about Luke a long time ago. Now, being the newest billionaire on *Forbes*'s list, he lived in a whole different world. Particularly when he returned to Silicon Valley. She had seen pictures of his mansion and read about all the fancy electronic conveniences he had. He would go back to his world once he got his family ranch taken care of, and she wouldn't see him again, maybe ever. Worse, someday he might bring one of those gorgeous women to the ranch. Scarlett knew she should keep that prospect in mind.

And as much as it pained her, she had always known deep down that he had moved on and she would never be part of his life.

Luke gazed up at the twinkling stars. One of the things he had always loved about being on the ranch—no city lights to hide the beauty of the night sky. He saw the stars, but his thoughts were on Scarlett. He wanted her in his arms and was disappointed she wouldn't sleep beside him. If she had, they would have had more kisses.

His pulse quickened. Remembering the feel of her lips pressed so sweetly against his was going to keep him awake, which sucked since he was totally exhausted. What a way to kill his slight chance for some sleep here.

He had forgotten what a force she could be.

When he had drawn his pistol, he was just thinking of putting down a suffering, hopelessly injured horse. He never thought about Scarlett jumping up and confronting him, standing right in front of a pointed gun. Fortunately, he had the safety on, but for a split second, she had surprised him. And then he remembered it was Scarlett and he should have known better. She was fiercely protective of her animals—he didn't have to be around her since she became a vet to realize that. She had been that way when she was fifteen years old. Probably when she was four years old, too.

He smiled in the darkness and placed his hands behind his head. He'd been lucky in business and done well. He had gotten accustomed to people being at his beck and call and doing his bidding, and that especially held true for his female companions. His life was filled with his pick of pretty, flirtatious women saying yes to whatever he wanted. But now he was back at his childhood home, and right away Scarlett told him to get off her property and go to hell. His smile grew. If she didn't agree with him, she would let him know in no uncertain terms. And it would be not only "no," but "hell, no." Clearly she didn't have a qualm about telling him what to do and what he *wasn't* going to do.

His smile faded. He knew it was all kinds

of wrong, but he wanted to go out with her. He wanted to take her to bed and make love for hours. She was as off-limits to him as much as if she had married that oil jerk who walked out on her, but his heart obviously hadn't gotten the memo.

Luke thought of the three women he'd seen the most this past year—gorgeous women who were fun to be with, sexy in bed, with dream bodies. They would never give him trouble or tell him to go to hell. He had to forget Scarlett, and as soon as he returned to California, he would look these women up and go out with whichever one he enjoyed the most.

Luke groaned. He had about an hour and a half and then the sun would be up. But now that he had a chance to get some shut-eye, Scarlett still filled his every thought. She was like a powder keg with a short, lighted fuse. At the same time, she was hot, luscious, sexy enough to make his blood boil. Her kiss should send steam out his ears.

He ached to hold her, to make love to her, to ravish her from head to toe. But as much as he wanted her, he knew he couldn't seduce her. He'd hurt her when he left before, and he didn't want to do that again.

That thought moved sleep further away. Thoughts of making love to her conjured up images that would keep him up another hour, he was sure. He might as well just get up and go back to work.

"Damn, woman, either get out of my thoughts or into my bed so I can get over you one way or another," he ground out, all the while knowing neither were going to happen.

With a muttered curse, he got up, trying to be quiet and move carefully so he didn't shake the pickup as he crawled out and went to work.

It was almost 9:00 a.m. when he returned to the pasture where he had parked and he saw Scarlett. She picked up her bag and approached him. Just watching her walk toward him turned him on. She had a sexy sway to her hips and an enticing walk. Wind caught locks of her hair and blew them across her forehead. He pushed his brown Resistol to the back of his head and waited.

"I've looked over all the livestock. You really are a miracle worker—the horses are on their feet. It may be my imagination, but they all look better, too." He grinned down at her. "How're you doing this morning with less than two hours' sleep?"

"I'm fine," she said, turning her back on him as she stepped up to a black horse to run her hands over it.

"When you're ready, I'll drive you home, Scarlett. You've been a fantastic help, and you've saved these horses. Whenever you have it ready, give me the bill."

"Sure." She peered up at him, her brow furrowed with concern. "You didn't get much sleep either. You were already up and gone when I got up."

"Yeah," he said, not wanting to tell her that he hadn't slept a wink after their smoking-hot kiss.

"I'll work for about an hour more, and then I think you'll be able to take care of them with no problem."

With a sigh, he moved on, going back to his truck to start making some calls now that it was morning. He needed to hire all sorts of people as quickly as possible to start getting the ranch up and running again.

An hour later he looked up to see Scarlett approaching.

"I think you can take me home now," she said. "At least until you find some more animals. Here's my bill."

He took the bill without even looking at it, his fingers brushing hers. He saw the flicker in her eyes, felt his own pulse jump in return. How could she do that to him? Even after all these years, she caused a chemical reaction in him from just barely having contact with her.

"I've been making calls and have already got someone hired to get a crew out here to start working. This afternoon I have an appointment to talk to a highly recommended Dallas contractor about the house. But those are my problems…nothing you need to concern yourself with." He squeezed her shoulder. "Come on, how about I take you to breakfast before dropping you at your place?"

"Thanks, but I just want to go home. Mom will have breakfast for me. I want a hot bath, and then I'm going to get some sleep."

"Okay, home it is," he said, taking her arm and smiling at her. "I need to check into the Bellamy Resort. After a night in the back of my truck, I'm ready for a five-star resort."

She drew a deep breath, and the moment he touched her, he was aware of another sizzle that ignited desire. He released her arm and turned away. Scarlett was off-limits, and he couldn't even touch her in the most casual way without having a physical reaction.

He held the door of his pickup, and when she climbed in, his gaze swept over her long legs clad in tight jeans. As he drove, he thought again about what an amazing job she had done with the animals and his chest swelled with appreciation.

"Everyone says you're the best vet in this part of the state," he praised. "And now I can see why."

"Thanks, Luke." She smiled and then turned to look out the window. They rode in companionable silence for several minutes before she glanced back toward him and asked, "So when are you planning on seeing your dad?"

"I think I need to wait a day or two until I won't lose it over the way he abandoned the ranch without telling me. If he had just clued me in, things would not have gotten so bad." He blew out an angry breath. "And I still don't know why none of the men who worked for him didn't let me know what was going on. He must have really ticked them off."

"He might have told them you were coming to take over, and they figured you knew."

"I hadn't thought of that." He hesitated. "I'm here not only to see about the ranch, but I have other matters to take care of, too. I'm going to see Will today."

She gave him a startled look. "Really? I have to say, I'm surprised to hear that. You're pretty removed from Royal and all that goes on here."

"Will and I've always stayed in touch and he's been out to see me a couple of times."

"I guess when I stop to think about it, you two were good friends."

"It's the damnedest thing about Will coming home to his own funeral. Quite a shock, right?"

She nodded. "You've got that right. This deal with Will—some of us know a few things, but not much. He is staying pretty hush-hush about the whole thing. But if you're seeing Will, I'm sure he'll bring you up to date on what's happened. Will's close friends apparently know some things. Like my brother, Toby."

"People in certain professions hear more secrets—people like hairstylists, bartenders—how about veterinarians?"

She laughed softly, and it was a sound that made him smile and he wanted to hear that beautiful laugh again. "I don't think so. My furry, four-legged regulars have very little to say to me, except to convince me they're glad to see me. I don't have to have any proof of that."

"I'll bet you've never been bitten by one of your patients."

"No, I haven't," she said. "They kind of melt when they come to the hospital. The ones that come to board go to a different section, and they're happy campers. We're happy to see them, too."

"You like your job, don't you?" he asked, but he already knew her answer.

"I love my job," she said, and he could hear the enthusiasm in her voice and knew that she felt the same about her work that he did about his.

"Lots of changes for me to come back to."

"I'm sorry about the Double U. I know that was a shock yesterday. I still can't believe your family place got so bad that the animals were just left to starve and die." She sighed. "I think it probably went downhill fast after your dad had to go to the hospital and then the assisted-living facility."

"Our family attorney helped with all that. You know Fred Sweeney?"

"Mr. Sweeney…sure. So how is your dad?"

"They're trying to get him dried out, and he's resisting. Nothing new there." He grimaced. "We've been down that road before."

"Sorry, Luke."

"Just be thankful for your family, Scarlett."

"I am," she murmured quietly. "If you find more horses and need my help, let me know."

"You were great last night. You passed on breakfast, but let me take you to Dallas to dinner Friday night. I owe you that much," he said, suddenly wanting a night with her and knowing he did owe her big-time for what she did last night.

She glanced at him and looked away, drawing a deep breath that made him glance down as her shirt hugged her curves. "Thanks, Luke, but you don't need to do that, and I have plans."

He didn't think she really had plans, but suspected she didn't want to go out with him. He nodded. "Sure, Scarlett. I owe you, though. You saved horses for me."

"That's my job."

He slowed and stopped in front of her house and came around to open her door, but she had already stepped out and gathered her things. She looked amused. "You don't need to walk me to the door. This isn't a date. I'll see you, Luke. Call if you have sick animals."

"Scarlett, you saved those horses. Your bill doesn't cover half of what you did. Let me do something to repay you. Can I make a donation to your business to help with abandoned animals?"

She nodded. "I'll take you up on that one. I'm on the web, so you can get my address and send a check. We take in dogs, cats, horses, occasionally other animals, even birds. We can always use more money to feed and care for them and advertise to get them placed in good homes."

"You're a softie for anything furry and four-footed."

They looked at each other, and for an instant he wanted to draw her into his arms. This was another goodbye between, them and he didn't like it. It shouldn't make any difference at all, but it did. That was just one more shock since he had returned to Royal. He should be able to walk away from Scarlett without batting an eye after all this time, so why was this simple goodbye so damned difficult?

"Bye, Scarlett. Thanks again."

She nodded. "Sure." She turned and went up her porch steps, and he headed back to climb into his pickup to leave. He looked in the rearview mirror and saw her standing in the doorway. She glanced over her shoulder at him and then went inside and closed the door.

He wondered whether he would see her again while he was in Royal. They had no future together and no reason to cross paths again. His parents' bad genes haunted him and because of that, he wasn't the man for Scarlett.

He drove to the new elegant five-star resort and was relieved to be in luxurious surroundings with instant service. Even before he showered, he made an appointment for his own PI from Dallas to come check the suite for bugs or hidden cameras because of the ongoing investigation of the attempt on Will's life, the funeral supposedly for Will, the disappearance of Rich Lowell and Jason Phillips, as well as the disappearance of money. He intended to work with Will's PI, but he didn't want Will's PI seen at the Bellamy where he was staying.

When the Dallas PI finished, Luke gave him instructions and had him check into a room in his name in the nearby small town of Brinkly. The PI was to leave the key with the concierge for Luke to pick up when he arrived later to meet with Will's PI, Cole Sullivan.

Luke ordered breakfast sent up and headed for his shower. This afternoon he would meet with Cole Sullivan. If they could find where the money went, they might begin to get some answers to the disappearance of Rich Lowell and Jason Phillips. As the hot water sluiced over him, washing away the dirt and grime of the last several hours, he released a frustrated breath... Whose ashes did they have when they had the funeral for Will? Ashes that were supposed to be Will's until he showed up alive and well at his own funeral.

Questions came to mind that Luke wanted answered. Questions for Cole Sullivan, questions for Will. And though it shouldn't be, the biggest question hovering in his thoughts was, would he see Scarlett again?

Three

Luke had time before the meeting with Cole. He dressed in jeans, a brown-and-red-plaid Western-style shirt, brown boots and a Stetson. He wanted to blend with the other men in Royal, and this Western attire would do the trick unless someone was specifically looking for him.

After climbing into his pickup, he drove a few short blocks to the bank where he kept an account. The bank president, Jeff Kline, had been a friend since high school, although he was two years older than Luke. Having grown up in Royal, Luke knew most people, which made doing business with them easier. When his meeting at the bank was over, Luke headed down to City Hall to meet with Sheriff Nathan Battle.

Luke had grown up knowing Nathan. They

shook hands, and Nathan motioned for Luke to have a seat. Luke pulled a check out of his pocket and extended it. "This is for the Double U, the back taxes, everything. If you need more, let me know, but this is what you wrote to me that Dad owed. I've been to the bank, and Double U is now in my name, and my father is no longer an official part of it. I hate to do that, but you've seen how he left it."

Nathan looked at the check, wrote a receipt and got out a file. "This is the right amount, and I'll give you that lien and auction notice, and this should ensure you keep the Double U. It was a fine ranch the years you were growing up. I'm glad to know you'll stay connected with us in Royal, and I hope we see you at the Texas Cattleman's Club sometime."

"I don't know how much I'll be back. I'm hiring good people to run the Double U, and if you have any suggestions, please let me know. Here's a list of the men I'm talking to. Do you know any of them?"

Nathan took the list and scanned it. "I do. I know all of them except this Chet Younger. I can look him up if you want."

"Thanks, but I can check him out."

Nathan laughed, crinkles forming at the corners of his dark brown eyes. "I guess you can. And you'll probably get better info than the Royal Police Department can dredge up. Well, I hope you come back here to live."

"I won't do that any time soon. I have West-Tech, and I love my work." He smiled amicably at the other man. "Nathan, thanks for your call. Scarlett McKittrick came out and tended to the animals that had survived until I got home. She's a miracle worker because I didn't expect her to save half of them, but I think they'll all make it."

"She's good and she's another one who loves her job. I'm sorry, Luke, about your dad."

"Well, he drank himself into it." Luke stood and folded the papers, putting them in his shirt pocket. "I'm damn glad to have the ranch out of debt. I just couldn't bear to see it go to auction. What a hell of a thing."

"It won't now. It's your ranch, free and clear, and it looks as if you'll get it back in great shape."

"I hope. It's good to be home in a lot of ways."

Nathan walked Luke to the door. "When you have time, maybe we can meet at the diner and have lunch."

"Sure. Thanks again, Nathan. You saved the Double U by your call."

Luke left, feeling better. The Double U was his again, and he felt he had taken the first step toward salvaging the ranch and eventually making it one of the best in Texas.

Moreover, his father's bills at the assisted-living center had been paid and arrangements made for Luke to take care of his father's bills from this point forward.

He returned to the Bellamy where he changed into a pale blue dress shirt and navy slacks. Promptly at 11:00 a.m., Will Sanders stepped into Luke's suite, and the two shook hands. Luke gazed into his friend's green eyes and smiled as he closed the door behind him. "I'm glad to see you alive and well."

"Just one more big shock in my life. Thanks for coming, Luke. If you can help follow the money trail, I think we might unravel a lot of the mystery."

"I'll do my best, Will. I'll meet with Cole Sullivan this afternoon and get started."

Luke listened to Will talk briefly about all that had happened to him, and how one thing after another pointed to Rich Lowell passing himself off as Will.

"To avoid compromising the investigation, not many people know all the details of what I've told you. I'm cooperating every way I can with the police, and I've informed them I have my own PI to help move things along."

Luke nodded. "You can count on me to keep

your confidence, Will. I know how much is at stake for you."

"Thanks for getting involved in my problems, which touch a lot of lives here. In addition to trying to track Rich down, I'm also concerned about Jason Phillips's disappearance. It isn't like him to just vanish, and it really isn't like him to lose contact with his daughter, Savannah. His brother, Aaron, is filling in to help take care of little Savannah, who's only six. Jason's sister, Megan, is helping, too. She and Aaron take turns." He blew out a breath. "They're worried, and rightfully so, about Jason. The more we find out about Rich, the worse it looks."

"I'm still trying to wrap my brain around this, so I can only imagine how his loved ones must be feeling."

Will nodded grimly. "And you might as well know—Megan received the urn with the ashes, presumably *my* ashes, because she was supposedly my wife. There was a note about how I died. They've sent the note for handwriting analysis, so we should get an answer any time now on that. They are also testing the ashes' DNA." His mouth hardened into a tight line. "We'll get answers sooner or later. I just don't want anyone else hurt." He ran his hand over his short black hair.

"Everyone is reeling from Rich's deceit. As you know, he and I grew up together."

"That's part of why he could get away with impersonating you. He knows everything about you,"

"I feel such a sense of betrayal. Rich wasn't poor. He was well-off. What would cause him to go to such extremes?"

"Greed. He wasn't as wealthy, and he wasn't the golden boy that you've always been," Luke said. "Most friends are happy for your wealth and success. Rich must have envied it beyond anything any of us could imagine."

"I suppose," Will said, shaking his head. "It's still shocking."

"Yeah. Life is filled with shocks."

Will nodded. "Sorry. I've just been thinking about my problems. I hear you have plenty of your own."

"I'm working on them. I paid off the ranch today, and I own it free and clear now. I can't believe how my dad left it. Rich Lowell was after money. My dad was after booze. It's pitiful, Will. I'm scared someday I'll be like him."

"You'll never be like your dad, Luke. Not ever," Will said, shaking his head and smiling. "You can relax on that one. You're a straight arrow filled with brilliant ideas and a great ability. Stop worrying about following in your dad's footsteps."

"I hope to hell you're right. Well, I'll talk to your PI and I'll see what I can come up with. If we can get proof of Rich taking some of that stolen money, then you can nail the bastard."

"Thanks again, Luke. I'll let you know if I learn anything, and you do the same for me. I'm telling you, watch your back. Rich tried to murder me."

"Even though I've know that, it still shocks me. I'll be careful."

"If we can pick up the money trail, that will be amazing." Will reached out and clapped his friend on the shoulder. "By the way, congratulations on making the *Forbes*'s list. Their newest billionaire—that's great."

"Thanks, buddy. But to be honest, I came home to a passel of trouble, and Silicon Valley and that list seem far removed from Royal, Texas. If I can help here, though, I'll be very happy. Money is paper, and it does leave a trail. And if Lowell took TCC money, we ought to be able to get some information about it."

"Rich has to have bank accounts, has to have places he keeps money and gets money."

Luke nodded in agreement. "My days will be pretty much filled with ranch business, but I can work on this at night if you or Cole can provide me with whatever information you have about the thefts."

"Thanks again, buddy. I know you already have a lot on your plate. I can't tell you how much I just want to look Rich in the eye and ask how he could do such a thing. Hurting so many people the way he did." He blew out an angry breath. "I shouldn't even have survived when he pushed me overboard off the yacht, but fortunately, I was rescued. I still have blocks of time I don't remember."

"We'll catch him, Will. We just have to."

After they said their goodbyes, Luke closed the door behind Will and made some calls. About thirty minutes later, he went downstairs and climbed into his pickup, driving south out of Royal to the scheduled rendezvous in Brinkly with the PI.

Promptly at one, Luke opened the door to the hotel suite, and Cole Sullivan stepped inside, introducing himself. Luke shook hands with the blue-eyed investigator who had once been a Texas Ranger.

"Thanks for driving to Brinkly," Luke said. "I felt we would have a lot better chance of having a private meeting here instead of Royal."

"I agree. I know you met with Will before lunch, and that's good."

"I'm all set up. Come pull up a chair and let me show you this new antifraud software we have."

"My business changes by the day, and I have the feeling I'm going to learn something new now."

"I hope I can help you catch Rich. We've all grown up together, and we know each other well. We know habits, sayings, mannerisms."

Cole nodded. "If we can pick up the money trail, you should be able to find Rich."

"It can't be a minute too soon."

As they talked, Luke had already set up his things, getting ready to look at what figures and information Cole had unearthed. The two men worked together for an hour, making arrangements for Cole to get information to Luke and set up how and when they would keep in touch.

When Cole left, Luke packed up his things to go back to Royal. He had three interviews already set up to hire a man to run the ranch. He also had two interviews to hire a contractor to build another ranch house. As soon as he reached Royal, he bought a black sports car and had it delivered to his hotel.

That night back in Royal, over a solitary dinner in his hotel room, for a moment he was lost in a vivid memory of holding Scarlett in his arms and kissing her. She had kissed him back, a fiery kiss that was a challenge and an invitation at the same time. He wanted her in his arms again. He shouldn't kiss her or even see her again, but he couldn't shake her out of his thoughts. Why did it seem so damn good to be with her?

He wanted to call her, ask her out, go have a fun evening, bring her back to his hotel and make love all night long. That was a dream and about as likely to happen as Rich Lowell appearing in Royal and surrendering to the police for his misdeeds.

Scarlett was probably back to not speaking to him and would tell him again to get off the McKittrick ranch. Luke blew out an exasperated breath. He needed to put Scarlett out of his thoughts, get done what he came to do and go home to California where he really fit in better. With his family, his genes, he would never be the man for Scarlett. Why was it so impossible to forget her?

He woke shortly before 6:00 a.m. the following morning. His phone was buzzing. He picked up and heard Will.

"We need a clandestine emergency meeting at my ranch today. Can you get out here by eleven?"

"I'll be there."

"Thanks. I want you here so I can fill you in on what's going on. We have to keep this meeting quiet, so don't breathe a word of it to anyone, okay?"

"Will do, and I'll see you." Putting aside his phone, Luke stretched and sat up. He'd slept in because he usually was up by 5:00 a.m., maybe a carryover from living on a ranch a lot of his life and getting up early. His schedule was blown to hell anyway after staying up all night at the Double U.

He wondered what had happened to cause Will to call a meeting. Well, he would know soon enough, he supposed. He also wondered how the animals were doing. He needed to get out to the Double U. He had talked several times to the man in charge of the crew of cowboys who were working on the ranch temporarily. Also, he had a contractor with a crew that would start work today. They would demolish the house he had grown up in, and he had seen this done before to homes in Silicon Valley. The house and any trace of it would be gone in hours. He'd have a vacant lot.

Did he want to rebuild in the same spot? He thought about the big trees on the property. There was a live oak that he suspected was well over one hundred years old. He thought it would be best to just rebuild where the original house had stood.

He wasn't in a hurry, but the sooner he could get good people hired, the sooner he could let go and let someone else take charge of the Double U and get back to the home he loved in Silicon Valley.

Once again his thoughts drifted back to Scarlett. No matter how hard he tried to concentrate on other things, she was always first and foremost in his mind. A grin spread across his face. He would drive out and check on the livestock, and if he had any sick animals he was calling her. First, because he wanted to see her. Second, she was a miracle worker where his livestock were concerned.

She'd always had a way with animals and had never been afraid of any of them. He remembered seeing her as a kid walk up to a snarling, growling, injured dog that was in pain and had its teeth bared. Smiling, he remembered how he kept telling her to get back, but she just went ahead and knelt by the dog, speaking softly, holding out her hand with a treat. She started singing, and the dog stopped growling and looked at the treat and took it. When he did, Scarlett gave him a shot so fast that Luke could barely believe his eyes. In seconds, the dog calmed, and she picked it up, put it in a carrier and off she went.

Later, he asked where she got the painkiller and when she learned how to give animals shots. She gave him one of her smug looks and said that she was studying to be a veterinarian and she had learned how and where to give a dog a shot for pain. Scarlett worked one day a week when she was fifteen for the local vet, and she obviously was a quick learner.

Still smiling over the memory, Luke shook his head, thoughts of her still prevalent in his mind as he carried on with his morning routine.

At 11:00 on the dot, he drove up to Will's house

at the Ace in the Hole Ranch, one of the finest spreads in Texas—which made Luke think about the ruin his father had brought to the Double U.

Other cars were parked in the drive, and he wondered how many knew the truth about what was happening. A butler showed Luke where everyone was gathering. With a firm handshake and friendly green eyes, Will welcomed Luke.

"It's good that you're here, buddy. I talked to Cole, and he's here, as well. He thinks this money trail is going to really help."

"I hope so. As I said before, I'll do my best."

Will gave him a crooked smile as he shook his head. "Thanks. I can't ask for better than that."

"I hope this meeting helps shed some more light on the case."

"Yeah, me, too. Thanks for coming on such short notice."

"No problem. I'll go say hello to the others."

"Sounds good. We'll start in just a minute."

It was easy to spot Aaron Phillips's dark hair and broad shoulders on the other side of the room, so Luke began to head that way, saying hello to others as he went. Toby McKittrick was present, standing across the room, and if looks could kill, Luke was certain he'd be a dead man. He nodded at Scarlett's big brother, seeing ice in Toby's aqua eyes before Toby turned away.

Luke couldn't be angry with Toby for being rude because Toby was protective of his family. Luke would always be sorry for hurting Scarlett but the alternative—if he had proposed to her when she was sixteen—would probably have brought Toby after him with a shotgun and dire warnings to get out of her life. Luke couldn't regret not getting engaged to Scarlett back then. He hadn't been ready for marriage at eighteen, and he didn't think Scarlett was at sixteen, even though she thought she was.

He moved around the room, greeting friends from his high school days and earlier. Nearly all the men in the room were members of the Texas Cattleman's Club, and Nathan Battle was among those present.

"Nathan, thanks again. If I'd lost the ranch at an auction, that would have been a horrible blow."

"Forget it. You own the Double U now, and it's in your name, so that takes care of losing the ranch. Good luck with the restoration. If anybody can get it done, you can."

"Thanks." Luke smiled and moved on to greet Aaron, Jason's brother.

"I'm sorry your brother is missing, Aaron."

"Thanks, Luke," he said, turning worry-filled eyes on Luke. "That's why this meeting has been called. They've turned up some new information.

You'll hear about it in just a minute. I guess the only good news here is now we know a little more and we have an answer."

"I've come home to all kinds of problems, my own with my dad and all this with Will walking into his own funeral."

"Yeah. Welcome home," Aaron remarked drily. "I'm sorry about your dad being sick."

"Thanks. We won't start on what all my dad has done. Take care, Aaron."

He moved on to greet Rand Gibson, second in command to Will at Spark Energy Solutions, an oil, gas and solar energy company that Luke knew had been extremely successful.

"Congratulations on making *Forbes*'s list," Rand said, shaking hands with Luke.

"Thanks. I'm doing what I love, and I suppose you are, too."

Before Rand could answer, Will spoke above the sounds of everyone talking. "I think we better call this meeting to order. Thank you for coming on such short notice.

"I'd like to get this meeting started because it was called suddenly and I know I've interrupted plans and schedules. It won't take long," Will said. "Well, for starters, Cole Sullivan, the PI I hired, has discovered that Jason has actually been kidnapped and may be in grave danger. He encourages anyone with information regarding the case to step forward so they can work to bring Jason home." He looked around the room. "If there is anyone here who has information, please talk to the police or Nathan. Even if it seems insignificant, if you know something about Rich or Jason, please let the authorities know."

Nathan waved his hand. "Right now, all we can do is hope and pray that Jason is still alive out there," he added.

Luke thought of the urn of ashes at Will's fake funeral. It was beginning to look as if those ashes might belong to Jason.

How could Rich Lowell, who had grown up with all the men in the room, betray those friendships in such a terrible way? No one could answer that question.

When the meeting adjourned, Luke left to go to the Double U ranch to meet with Abe Ellingson, his new builder, and Reuben Lindner, the man he had hired to run the ranch, so the three of them could go over what needed to be done and what Luke wanted.

He spent the next three hours talking to the builder about the house and the outbuildings. Reuben left to go back to Royal to set up interviews to hire cowboys to work at the Double U.

When his meeting with the builder was finished, Luke fed and checked the livestock. In less than an hour he found a sick calf. He knew it was a case for Scarlett, so he sent her a text. Luke felt an uncustomary sense of loss, albeit a feeling he'd had several times since returning to Texas. How could his father let everything go to hell like this—starving animals, a rising debt—all to drink himself senseless? Luke thought of Scarlett. If he was the last man on earth, he didn't deserve her and shouldn't get entangled in her life. Suppose he turned out like his father someday?

When Luke got no text answer and couldn't get Scarlett by phone, he climbed into his pickup to drive to the McKittrick ranch. As he approached the house, he spotted two women rocking on the porch. When he stepped out of his pickup and headed toward the house, the dogs came running, so he paused to pet some of them and let them calm down. The dogs followed as he walked toward the porch. His gaze flitted over Mrs. McKittrick and then swept more slowly over Scarlett, and he was startled by what he saw. Seated in a rocker facing her mother, Scarlett held a baby in her arms.

Waving to him, Joyce McKittrick went inside the house. He climbed the steps and walked to Scarlett, his pulse beating faster. Why did she always look so good to him? Dressed in a red T-shirt that fit her gorgeous curves and snug jeans, Scarlett rocked the little baby.

Knowing nothing about babies, Luke looked at a little boy with thick, curly black hair, big, long-lashed, soulful brown eyes and beautiful, golden-brown skin. Luke gave the bigger dogs a cursory pat and walked up to Scarlett. "Are you babysitting?" He'd heard Toby and Naomi had a little girl, so it wasn't her niece.

As she gave him a level look, Scarlett raised her chin. "No, I'm not babysitting. This is my baby boy, Carl."

Flabbergasted, Luke looked at the infant again. "He's yours?"

"He's my adopted baby. I can't have children of my own, Luke."

Stunned, he looked at the baby and then at her. Why hadn't someone mentioned Scarlett's baby when he'd been told that she had been engaged until the guy walked out on her?

"Why a baby, Scarlett?" he blurted, still staring at the little guy.

"I thought I was going to get married and we wanted a baby, so we started adoption proceedings. It takes time to adopt a baby, just as it takes time to have a baby. Tanner walked out and the marriage was off, but then Carl came up for adoption shortly after he left. I think Tanner went to Chicago. I lost track of him." She tenderly stroked her baby boy's head. "It just seemed like it was meant to be. The agency approved the adoption, I went through the legal process and I'm now a single mom."

He heard the note of challenge in her voice and stopped staring at the baby to look at Scarlett. "Congratulations seems inadequate. That fits you, Scarlett. You collect animals to care for. Why not a baby?" he remarked, his surprise diminishing fast after her explanation. It was so like Scarlett to adopt a baby if she could. She was a caregiver deluxe, and it spilled over in all aspects of her life.

"Why are you here, Luke?" she asked, a cold note in her tone.

"Oh, damn, I forgot. I've got a really sick calf and I can't help him—"

Instantly, Scarlett stood and handed the baby to Luke. "I'll get my things. Hold Carl for a minute," she said. "Watch him until I get back."

Luke couldn't recall holding a baby in his life. "Scarlett, I can't—"

"Sure, you can. He doesn't bite. He only has one tooth," she flung over her shoulder as she disappeared through the door, and he was certain she was laughing.

He blinked and looked down at the little baby she had thrust into his arms. He was holding Carl underneath each arm. Realizing that wasn't any way to hold a baby, Luke sat and put the little boy in his lap.

"Hi, Carl," he said, smiling, his heart pounding with fear that he would frighten the little fellow. "Dammit, Scarlett—whoops, sorry, Carl. Thank goodness, you're too little to repeat words. Your mama would be unhappy with me. I'm glad I don't scare you." He smiled at Carl again, and when the baby smiled back at him, a dimple showing in his cheek. Luke felt as if his heart melted.

"Hey, Carl, you're a cute kid," he praised, suddenly feeling at ease with the little guy. "You're not screaming or crying or making angry faces. You must not even care that I don't know zip about babies."

Carl giggled and Luke laughed, making Carl giggle again. Scarlett stepped back outside.

"Well, look at you, Mister Doesn't-Know-Anything-About-Babies. You've got him giggling and laughing and happy as all-get-out."

"He doesn't know he's with a terrified man who has never held a baby before."

"Then it is time you did, and Carl is a good one to practice with. You're doing fine. You get an A for amazingly okay." She smiled at him, and, as he smiled in return, Luke's heart thudded.

He remembered the fun moments with Scarlett when they dated in high school, the laughter that came so easily. He felt an ache in his gut. This moment, laughing with Scarlett, holding her baby on his lap, felt so right—which was ridiculous. He was *not* interested in babies, families, getting tied down, and it could never work with Scarlett. Even if he wanted it, she didn't. She was barely civil to him unless it involved animals and now her baby, Carl.

"I always figure babies and animals sense when someone is afraid of them or doesn't know what to do. He doesn't seem to care."

"He likes you," she said, laughing again. "You're good daddy material, Luke. Who would've guessed?"

"Scarlett," he snarled, teasing her because she was teasing him. "I'm not daddy material in any way, shape or form. Forget that."

She leaned closer, batting her eyes at him, teasing and flirting with him as her voice thickened, "I'm not about to forget that very appealing aspect of your personality."

He drew a deep breath. "Scarlett, you're just asking for trouble."

Laughing, she took Carl from him and stepped away."

"Let me give Carl to Mom, and then we can head out. I can drive and you won't—"

"Forget it. I'm here. I'll take you to the ranch and bring you back."

She nodded and left to hand Carl off to her mother. Once again, he remembered old times with her, fun times when she was carefree, flirty and oh, so sexy. He wiped his brow. She had too easily fanned flames between them.

He was still amazed that Scarlett had a baby. He was a cute kid and a happy little baby, which made life easier. It had actually been a fun few minutes, and that surprised him. He couldn't recall holding a baby, and he wouldn't have thought he could keep one happy five seconds.

In minutes, Scarlett reappeared. "Ready to go?"

"Sure am. And thank you, Scarlett. You're coming to my rescue again. I really need you this time, too. This little calf is so dang sick. I don't know whether it'll be alive when we get there, but I had to try," he said.

"I'll do everything I can to help him, Luke. I promise you that."

"I never doubted that for a moment." He smiled at her. "Scarlett, pick out two of the reliable big mutts that we can take with us for watchdogs tonight. Unless you have to be back here for your baby, I have a feeling you may be sitting up all night. You and I will be on the ranch alone, and Milt Dawson, the man in charge of the cowboys, said last night there were vandals who just messed stuff up. He's bringing lights and part of the crew will start staying at night after tonight. If you're scared, I'll bring you home, but he said it's only vandalism, so it's probably kids. Nothing big. I can run anyone off."

"I don't doubt that and I'm not scared. I may be up with the calf."

"If we can, I want to sleep in peace and not have to keep one eye open for someone sneaking up. Do you have two big dogs we can take with us?"

"Oh, my, yes."

She whistled and more than a dozen came on the run. She picked out four and got them in the back of the pickup with minimal effort. "We're ready. It was that easy, and you can trust that you have four watchdogs."

He laughed. "You could be an animal trainer, too. Very talented woman."

"I just know them, and they know me. They're smart and they do what I want."

"I would, too, if you'd scratch my belly and pet me," he said, leering at her, and she had to laugh.

"You can't resist, can you? Some things never change."

"You bring out my wicked side," he drawled, and reached out to give her a quick, impersonal hug.

It should have been impersonal, but it wasn't

for him at all. He held the pickup door for her. As she passed him to climb in, he caught a scent of perfume, something exotic, making him think of holding her and kissing her. His gaze slid down the length of her, the tight jeans over her trim ass, her long legs. For a long, heated moment, he wanted her with all his being. Common sense reminded him that was not going to happen. She slid onto the seat, and he closed the door, drawing a deep breath, wishing he could at least kiss her once more. Only he would want more than once. Right now, he wanted a night of endless kisses.

"I'm glad you're trying to save the calf," she told him when he was in the pickup and headed toward the county road.

"I found a small herd in that canyon on the far west side of the ranch. This calf looks about a week old. The mother isn't in great shape, but both of them and a dozen others have survived. For once, mama isn't trying to run me off. She either senses I'm trying to help her baby, or she's too sick and weak herself to try to chase me away."

"Oh, my. She's really sick. We'll do what we can."

"Thanks for coming on such short notice," he murmured, thinking how polite they were with each other. She hadn't been cautious and polite when he'd kissed her the other night, however. His pulse jumped at the thought, and he wondered if he would get the chance to kiss her this time. He had a feeling she would stay the night to sit with the calf if need be.

"No problem."

"I own the ranch now," Luke added. "I paid off Dad's debts, the mortgages, the loans and the incredible bills. I'll bet guys left here without their pay. Some of them may have taken livestock to make up for missing pay, and I hope they did. It bothers me that Dad might not have paid guys that worked for him. We used to have good guys that did a fine job.

"I've already hired a man to run the place. Reuben Lindner. He came with all kinds of good qualifications. Do you know him?"

She shook her head. "No, but that doesn't mean much. I'm not a rancher."

"I've got a builder, too, Abe Ellison."

"That one I do know. He built my clinic. He's good at ranch buildings, barns and houses, too. You have an excellent builder, but that's no surprise. I think he does a lot of business in Dallas as well as in Royal."

"Soon they'll finish demolishing the house so they can start building a new one."

"One like you have in Silicon Valley?" she asked.

Surprised, he glanced at her. "How do you know about my Silicon Valley home?"

"It's been in magazines, and I've read about all the electronic gadgetry and amazing things for houses of the future."

"So you read about me?" he asked, surprised. Her cheeks flooded with pink and he wanted to reach out and put his arm around her.

"Sure, when I see something in a magazine or the paper about a former schoolmate, I usually read it," she said, looking out the window. "Thank you for the chance to save the calf. I'm glad you didn't just put it down."

"Maybe you can work some more of your magic."

"I'll try."

"You have a cute kid, Scarlett."

Her eyes sparkled with joy. "He's my whole world now. Mom adores him, too. All of us do. So does Toby. Carl's too little now, but eventually he and my brother's little girl, Ava, will play together."

"Your ex-fiancé didn't want kids?"

"Just the opposite. He comes from old money and was under a lot of pressure from his family to have a baby, an heir. When he found out I couldn't get pregnant, he almost broke up with me. So then we decided to adopt. But then the adoption proceedings began to drag out, and Tanner left. I debated with myself about taking my name off the list, and while I was thinking it over, the agency called. I've told you the rest."

"That must have been a difficult decision, deciding to raise a baby on your own."

"It was, but it was the best decision I ever made. Even though I'm a single mom, because of living with Mom and having Toby and Naomi close, they approved the adoption without Tanner. I'm so glad I went ahead. I love little Carl so much, and he's such a sweet blessing. I don't expect to have any more children."

"He's cute, all right." He winked at her. "It's just a shock to see you with a baby."

"I'm happy. Carl and my job are everything to me, Luke. I think I was meant to care for others and for animals. It's what I've done all my life."

"It's a good thing there are people like you in the world. The world needs your help."

"I have a good life," she said.

"We both do. You're doing your thing and love it, and I'm doing mine and I love it, as well."

"And never the twain shall meet—isn't that how an old saying goes?"

"I don't know about that old saying. My job is pretty much my whole life. Dad and I have grown apart through the years, which is sad, but that's the truth. He's the only one of my family left. I have no relatives."

"I'm sorry," she said, giving his wrist a squeeze. The minute she touched him, he felt a current buzz through him, and he took a deep breath. She released his wrist instantly, and her cheeks were pink again. She didn't glance his way, but her breathing was deeper and she had a reaction just as much as he did, which made him want her in his arms more than ever.

"Good or bad, no matter what you have, family is important. I feel like I should have done more but all I can do is go from here and try to make things better. I want to save the ranch and you're helping save the animals. That's a start."

Coming home isn't turning out to be what I expected. It's worse, but with your help, we've saved the surviving animals. I may lose this calf, but the rest seem mostly okay. None of the other animals are as sick as this calf."

"As I said, I'll do what I can."

He smiled. "You always do more than anyone could expect. While you're here, I'll check the livestock we've found and see if any others need your attention."

He turned in the familiar road that used to lead to his home. When they drove to the barn and parked to get out, he could hear the mother cow bawling. She stood in the corral by the barn. "She wants her baby," he said.

"I'll check her over and give her something to calm her. Let's look at the calf first, though. He may be critical."

The dogs stood in the back of the pickup, and she walked around to tell them to get down.

"They'll stay in whatever area I'm in," she told Luke. He smiled.

"I guarantee you, I would, too," he said and she shook her head, but she returned his smile.

Luke took her arm to lead her to the barn. He didn't need to hold her arm, but he couldn't resist reaching out to touch her. He ached to pull her into his arms and kiss her again. It was good to be with her and had seemed natural and right to be with her and baby Carl. He knew it was ridiculous for him to feel that way, but he couldn't help it.

He scowled. Scarlett hadn't even wanted him on their property, and she was only with him because she was such a softie for animals in trouble. She still felt something though, because she reacted slightly each time he touched her. He needed to think about the tasks he had to get done, but this darn woman was in his system and he had no clue how to stem these feelings.

His hand was clasped lightly on Scarlett's upper arm, sending waves of longing within him to turn her around, haul her against him and kiss her again. Another one of her bone-melting kisses that could make him shake with longing, almost explode into flames, and want to make out with her for hours.

"Luke, where's the calf?" Scarlett looked up at him, speaking loudly, and he realized she had asked him more than once.

"Sorry, I was lost in thought and memories about you and me and this barn," which he hadn't been, but he was now. He saw her faint blush.

"Keep your mind on today and the problems here. That was a long, long time ago. Forget it."

He leaned closer. "There's no way in hell I can forget a single moment I spent with you, especially if I was kissing you, and when we were in this barn, we were definitely kissing. If you don't remember, I can tell you exactly—"

"Don't you dare bring that up, Luke Weston!" She glared up at him. "Where's that sick calf?"

When Luke led her to a stall, she pushed ahead of him and knelt in the hay, opening her bag and bending over the calf.

"Text if you need me," Luke said. "I'm going to look and see if there are other animals I want you to check before you leave here."

"Sure," she said without looking up, and he wondered if she really even heard what he said.

He walked through the barn and remembered years earlier how they had made love several times in this very barn. He could remember it so clearly, and he guessed that she could, too.

For several long moments, he just stood motionless inside the barn, staring into space, thinking about Scarlett and lost in memories of making love. With a groan, he tried to get her out of his thoughts, focus on the animals that needed looking after. But it was impossible to shake taunting images and memories of times when he had held Scarlett in his arms, both of them naked while he had run his hands all over her, kissed her and spent hours making love to her.

Right or wrong, he wanted one night with her now. Was there a chance in hell of that happening?

Four

Scarlett worked swiftly. The calf was malnourished, ill and, like some of the other sick, weaker
horses and steers, wild animals had tried to bring it
down. It was dinner to them. She hoped she could
save the calf. She left to find the mama cow, and it
didn't take long to get something to quiet her. The
cow had cuts, too. Every weak or injured animal
was prey for wild animals, but Scarlett suspected
the mama cow had gotten attacked when she was
trying to protect her baby or fend off predators
that were after the calf.

Luke ordered dinner again, and they ate hamburgers about ten that night.

"I think the calf will make it through the night,
but I've sent Toby a text to come get the calf in the
morning first thing and get it to the Royal Veteri-

nary Hospital. It's been attacked, probably by coyotes, and I'm surprised it survived."

"That was probably its mama's doing. Even a pack of coyotes would think twice before taking her on in a fight." He met her gaze, and a smile flickered on his lips "I've said it before—you're a miracle worker with animals. I mailed you another check. You should get it tomorrow."

"You paid your bill."

"This is extra. Take it and use it to save some animals. You said that you take in the big animals, horses and cattle."

"Yes. I'll take any animal that's abandoned and needs help."

"Then you consider this check a donation and you cash it and use it to help the animals."

She smiled at him "Thanks, Luke. That's nice." He had a lantern that ran on batteries hanging from a rafter, and it shed a soft, golden glow over the stall. The calf was in the next stall, and they had moved to the adjoining one when they ate their burgers. She could hear the calf breathing and could tell what was happening from where she was.

A golden light spilled over Luke, and she couldn't resist reaching out to take his hand. "Thanks," she said softly. "Whatever you sent, it's welcome and will help some animals."

She released his hand just as quickly and knew she shouldn't touch him. However, the moment she started to take her hand off his, he placed his other hand over hers to keep her from pulling away. His hot, hungry gaze held her transfixed more than his hand, and her heart pounded with excitement. Too swiftly, she remembered being in his arms, recalled his kisses that could make her pulse race and set her ablaze with desire.

He was all she wanted, and he had hurt her so badly before. She never wanted to go through that kind of hurt again and she couldn't bear even a tiny bit of hurt for Carl, but it was Luke, and he was holding her hand, looking at her as if she were the only woman on earth, desire glimmering in his eyes. He stood and pulled her to her feet.

Common sense said to pull away, to move, to say no to him. She couldn't. She wanted him. Her gaze lowered to his mouth, and then she looked up to meet his eyes again.

"A kiss isn't going to hurt, Scarlett," he said in a husky, coaxing voice that was as sexy as a caress. Her heart throbbed as she looked at him, and, hard as she tried, she couldn't say no and couldn't move away.

"If we kiss, we won't be able to stop," she whispered. "I don't want to get hurt."

Something flickered in the depths of his eyes.

"A kiss—that's all. Just a kiss between old friends. You'll forget all about it," he said, drawing her to him.

And then she was in Luke's embrace, devoured by blue-green eyes, his delicious mouth hovering above hers. She wanted his kiss, wanted to kiss him in return. Common sense was a small voice of protest that faded fast beneath the hungry look he gave her. There was no mistaking his intention. When he leaned closer, her heart pounded until she thought he would hear it. She wound her arms around his neck, turned her face up and closed her eyes as his mouth brushed ever so lightly against hers.

Scarlett moaned, spinning in a swirl of desire, wanting him and wanting him to remember kissing her. She wanted to kiss him until he was as hot, as eager, as consumed with desire as she was. Holding her tightly against his hard, muscled body, he ran his hand down her back and over her bottom, pulling her up against him while he spread his legs and pressed her intimately against his thick erection.

He leaned over her, his tongue stroking hers, his kiss making her want to kiss him ravenously in return, until he wanted her more than he could remember ever wanting anyone. She wanted him to remember their kisses when he was back in Silicon

Valley in his glitzy, high-tech world. She didn't want him to walk away without remembering or looking back or realizing he might have shaken up his own world when he kissed her.

She ran her fingers through his hair while she thrust her tongue over his and shifted her hips slightly, moving against him, hearing him groan. Luke had taken her heart when she was sixteen years old. She thought she had gotten over him, but when he kissed her like this, she realized she had never gotten over him completely. He could walk back into her life, make her melt, set her on fire with longing and lust. She wanted to ravish every inch of him, and she wanted him to ravish every inch of her.

Scarlett knew the magic he could cause when he had been a kid in high school, and her heart thudded faster at the thought of making love with him now that he was a man. But if she did, she ran the risk of really falling in love with him. The deep, real kind of love that she couldn't get over. What mattered even more now—she didn't want Carl hurt. If Luke was really in her life, he would be in her baby's life, too. And Carl could so easily love Luke. She couldn't bear for Luke to break Carl's heart.

She had barely shed tears over Tanner walking

out and had chalked it up to being grown and not a high school kid.

But now she knew she hadn't cried over Tanner, because she hadn't really been in love with him. Sure, he was fun and exciting and they were compatible, but something had always been missing. That spark, that flame of passion that she was feeling right now in Luke's arms.

The thoughts spun through her mind as she kissed Luke, and then thoughts were gone and feelings took over completely. Desire overwhelmed her. Luke was holding her, kissing her until she couldn't think of anything except wanting more of him, of his hands, his mouth, his strong, muscular body, his thick, hard cock. She and Luke didn't belong together—there could never be marriage or anything lasting. There couldn't even be anything, except maybe tonight. How much would she get hurt if they made love once? How much would she get hurt if they *didn't*?

She didn't want to look back with longing or regret. Life was meant to be lived.

She moved her hips against him slightly again, rubbing his thick erection, sliding her hands down his back, down over his butt. He raised his head to look at her.

Desire darkened his blue-green eyes and made

her heart race. He wanted her, and she knew it when she looked into his eyes.

"Luke," she whispered just his name, but she meant more than that. In that whispered plea, she was telling him she wanted to make love tonight, to do all the things she had dreamed about. She slid her fingers around to unbutton the top buttons of his shirt and pull his shirt out of his jeans.

He already had the hem of her shirt in his hands, and he drew the shirt over her head and tossed it aside. She heard his gasp of pleasure as he looked down at her and unfastened her lacy bra to push it away. He cupped her breasts in his hands and groaned, a guttural sound of longing and approval.

"Beautiful," he whispered, running his thumbs lightly over her nipples. "Scarlett, you're so beautiful, so soft. I want you."

She reached up to slip her hand behind his head and pull him down to kiss him, running her tongue over his lower lip first, then darting it up to touch the corners of his mouth, before plunging deep inside when she pressed her mouth against his and kissed him passionately.

Her hands fluttered over his muscled chest, unfastening the buttons to push open his shirt, then drifted down to undo his big belt buckle and pull off his belt. While they kissed, she unbuttoned his jeans. As she pushed them away, he returned the favor and peeled off her jeans. She stepped back to hook her fingers in her lacy panties, drawing them down slowly while he watched her.

Scarlett stepped out of them, moving her hips in a slow circle as she took his thick rod in her hands to rub against her legs before she knelt to take him in her mouth, her tongue stroking him.

His fingers laced in her short hair, and he groaned as she slowly licked his hard erection, drawing her tongue over him while she held him with one hand and caressed him between his legs with her other.

She heard the sharp intake of his breath, which excited and satisfied her because she wanted to steal his breath, make him lose control, cause him to remember this night, to stir him up as he did her. He pulled her up to look into her eyes. She leaned forward placing her mouth on his to kiss him, her tongue thrusting slowly in and out of his mouth again. He held her tightly with one arm, his other hand caressing her, running reverently over her bottom.

He bent lower to circle her nipple with his tongue while he stroked her other breast, his hand a feathery caress that made her quiver as he brushed a taut peak.

She gasped, closing her eyes, shutting away everything except his hands, his mouth and his tongue on her, working magic. Or was it magic because it was Luke holding her and kissing her?

He walked away, rustling hay with each step, to reach up and pull down a horse blanket that he spread on the hay-covered dirt floor. He picked her up and knelt to place her on it, and then, as he stretched out beside her, he drew her into his arms and kissed her, another long, heated kiss that shut out the world and left only the two of them.

While they kissed, he caressed her, running his hands over her until he shifted and moved between her legs to trail his lips up the inside of her thighs, planting slow, wet kisses. His tongue slid over her, hot and wet, moving up, causing her to arch and spread her legs for him. Kneeling between them, he propped her legs on his shoulders, to give him access to her as his hands fluttered over her in light caresses, his fingers drifting on her thighs, stroking between her legs, making her writhe with desire.

As he ravished her, his tongue thrusting, going over her intimately, she arched her back with pure, wanton need, craving more of him. She wanted him inside her, but if they were going to make love, she didn't want to rush it, not after waiting all this time. The moment felt dreamlike because she had thought about it, imagined it, longed for it so many lonely, aching nights. But his hands and his mouth and his thick erection, his muscled body and strong arms weren't a dream. They were real for her to touch, caress, kiss, memorize and pleasure herself with.

Shifting away, he kissed her ankles, running his tongue over her, caressing her long legs, watching her shift as he touched her and her need heightened. He drifted higher and she could run her fingers in his hair, gasp with pleasure as his hands and then his tongue moved up her inner thigh, first one leg and then the other.

"Such long, long, gorgeous legs," he rasped, showering more caresses and wet kisses along her inner legs, inching higher, now a thrilling torment that made her want to spread her legs and draw him into her softness. He had moved up where she could kiss and caress him, stroking his manhood.

While his hands and tongue heightened desire and need, she closed her eyes, lost in sensations. She had yielded herself totally to him. She cried out, grasping his strong arms as he used his hands and his tongue to drive her wild.

"Luke, love me," she whispered. "I want you now."

"Wait, wait for more," he whispered while his fingers continued to rub, building her need, carrying her toward a climax.

As she kissed and ran her hands lightly over

him, she relished the moment. It was Luke in her arms, Luke kissing her, Luke taking her to paradise.

She tensed and clung to him, moving her hips furiously. "Luke, I need you now," she gasped, wanting him inside her, holding her, consuming her.

"It's too soon, Scarlett," he said, picking her up and putting her astride his lap, so she sat facing him with her legs spread apart to give him access to her.

"We're going to have some sexy fun. Hot, steamy, fun," he said, trailing kisses lower along her throat, down to her breast, to take it in his mouth and tease and run his tongue over her nipple.

He paused to look up at her as he cupped each breast in his hands. "You're breathtaking."

He toyed with her, with one hand between her legs and his other hand caressing her breast, while he kissed her and she stroked his erection.

With his arm around her neck, Luke pulled her close to kiss her passionately, his tongue exploring her mouth. She kissed him in return just as feverishly, hungry for more of him, wanting him more than ever.

He kissed her again, pulling her into his lap

while he ran his hands languorously over her. "You're gorgeous. You're perfect."

"I'm not, but I want you to continue to think that way. You won't need a condom. They said I can't get pregnant."

"We won't take chances," he answered. "We have a lot of catching up to do," he said, putting on the condom and moving between her legs. His gaze swept over her. "Tonight you're mine," he whispered with a hoarse, grating whisper.

He kissed away her answer and came down between her legs to enter her. She gasped with pleasure, crying out and holding him. His mouth covered hers as he entered her, filling her completely.

She clung to him, desire driving her now with all reasoning gone. She ran one hand down his back, over his firm bottom, moving her hips against him, while they rocked hard and fast. Everything about him felt powerful and masculine and potently sexy. And then she was lost and couldn't think about anything. Sensations swirled through her, and they moved faster, pumping wildly as she gyrated against him.

Suddenly, she climaxed. Waves of release and rapture washed over her when she moved with him, and then, dimly, she heard his low, guttural groan while he climaxed.

Still thrusting hard and fast, they moved together as ecstasy and joy swamped her. They both gasped for breath, their bodies glistening with sweat.

She clung to him as they slowed and began to breathe normally. Closing her eyes, she held him tightly. For this night, this hour, Luke was in her arms, loving her and letting her love him. This was her dream for so many lonely nights as a teen. When he left for California, she thought he had gone out of her life forever, and, in truth, he had. But for a few precious minutes tonight, her wishes had been partially fulfilled.

Realistically, she knew that this loving wouldn't last, and it was meaningless for both of them. There was no way he would ever truly love her or want her in his life on a permanent basis. She wasn't the woman for him in too many ways. But for tonight, she could forget the yesterdays and the tomorrows and just hold him and have hot, lusty rapturous sex with him.

"There's no woman on earth like you, Scarlett," he whispered and turned his head to kiss her lightly on her forehead.

"I could say the same about you. We're good together in bed."

"Damn good. I think you melted my bones."

She flashed him a coy smile. "I know one way to help you recuperate. I can see to that."

"I hope you do, but not quite yet. Let me catch my breath. This has to be the best night in my life in a long, long time. I hope the little calf survives—that would really make it the best night ever. It won't be quite the same if the calf doesn't make it."

She rolled over to pull out her phone. "Toby will be here at 6:30 a.m. to transport the calf to the Royal Veterinary Hospital."

Luke shifted to his side, still holding her close, showering light kisses on her temple, her cheek, her ear, her throat. "You're marvelous, Scarlett. Marvelous, sexy, hot. I've melted."

"I hope so," she said sweetly and smiled up at him. "This is crazy, Luke, and we'll both be sorry. *I'll* be sorry. You know I can't take sex lightly the way you do."

"Who said I do?"

"Give me credit for an ounce of sense," she scoffed. "This will be a roll in the hay, literally, for you and soon forgotten."

"If you think I'm going to forget the past hour for a long, long, long time, if ever, you are sorely mistaken."

"Time will tell." They grew silent, and she was content, trying to avoid thinking beyond the present moment. She was in Luke's arms, and it felt right, and it finally chased away the memories of the sad and angry moments between them. The euphoria, the closeness, their making love—none of it would last, but she would relish this night with him and, right now, she didn't want to think beyond it. She would be hurt again, but there was no way she could have said no to him tonight.

He held her close against him and she felt wrapped in euphoria and guessed that he did, too.

" You're an adorable mom," he said, turning his head to kiss her.

She wrapped her arm around his neck to hold him as she kissed him in return. Tonight was all about them, not the past, or what would happen in the future. Luke was once again in her arms, kissing her, loving her, and she had already crossed a line, so there was no going back now. She snuggled closer and pressed against him, feeling his hard erection thrust against her. He was ready for love again, and so was she.

Saturday morning, Luke opened his eyes to see Scarlett gathering her clothes. He closed his hand around her ankle, and she turned to look at him.

"Good morning, gorgeous," he said, smiling at her. "Come down here. And toss the clothes. I really like you naked."

She smiled in return as she gave a reluctant shake of her head. "You forget—we have a sick calf, and Toby will appear before you know it. He's up before the sun."

Luke groaned. "Your brother. I'm glad he's coming to get the calf, but he could give us a little time here."

"I doubt if my brother views us being together as good news."

"I'm lucky if he doesn't slug me."

"Toby would do no such thing," she insisted. "Well, at least not unless he's provoked by you. You're smart enough to avoid that."

He grimaced. "I hope to hell I am. How's the calf?"

"Still pretty sick. I hate to take it from its mama, but we have to. Right now I'm going to the house where I hope the water still works and I can take a shower."

Luke sat up and rubbed the back of his neck, stretching out his arms.

"Can I come with you? It'll save time if we shower together."

"I don't know how you can even say that with a straight face. If we get in a shower together, it isn't going to save time."

"Might," Luke said, standing and grabbing his clothes. "Let me show you," he drawled.

She pulled her shirt over her head, stepped into her jeans and pulled on her boots. "I'm dressing to get from here to the house. You better do the same, in case Toby drives up."

Luke nodded because she was right. He didn't want to leave the barn naked with her and run into her brother. In minutes they walked through the house that was almost devoid of furniture and had graffiti on some walls, broken windows—a standing trash heap was all he could call it. Luke tried to avoid thinking about what used to be and the years when he was young and very happy here.

Scarlett took his hand. "Luke, I'm sorry. I can't imagine how I would feel if this happened to our place."

"You don't ever have to spend one second imagining this in connection with your place. You have a super family. Toby's a fine guy and a good brother. Your mom is a rock for her whole family. You can always count on her, and she constantly showers all of you with love and affection. Your place is one of those oases in the world where it's a haven of love for the family."

"I have to agree. I just hope I can give that to Carl the way Mom gave us so much. But I'm sorry for what you're going through."

"Thanks. I'll go home to California and get on with life, and this will just be a bad memory I'll try to forget. Last night is what I'll remember. That makes up for a lot of hurt."

She was silent, and he wondered if he had hurt her again. He didn't feel he had because she was mature enough now to see his tainted family history for what it was. If he asked her to take him back, he was certain she would say no immediately. They weren't in love, and she wouldn't want to be any part of a family that let a ranch go to ruin like the Double U and abandoned the animals they owned.

To Scarlett, Luke knew he could never mean anything more than a fun night in bed with an old friend. She would never want to be seriously connected with a man like him. He really didn't blame her. He wished he could disconnect himself. He wouldn't ask her for a binding relationship because of the possibility he would turn into a man like his dad.

"It's good for everyone in this area that you're going to keep the ranch and rebuild. It'll thrive with you in charge, and you'll have a fine working ranch again." She patted his shoulder. "Just think about what will be, and try to let the past go."

"If I can keep my dad from wrecking it again. I don't really think he'll be back on the ranch, anyway. I'll get him a house in Royal if he wants one, but from the reports I'm getting, I don't think he'll ever be able to leave the facility where he is now, unless it's straight to the hospital." He told her all this because it was obvious she was trying to be sympathetic and thought he was quiet, lost in thoughts about his dad and the ranch. He didn't think he would get sympathy if she knew he had been thinking about the two of them.

Only there really wasn't any "two of them." He could never really be a part of Scarlett's life, and if he ever started thinking he could, all he had to do was remember the condition his dad had let the ranch sink into because of his drinking addiction.

"I have a beer, especially on hot days or out partying. I probably should cut the alcohol and view it like poison before I end up like my dad."

"You're not going to do that," she said. They had reached a bathroom with a working shower, and she turned to put her index finger against his chest.

"I get to shower first so I'll be ready to meet Toby."

Luke smiled at her and put his hand on the wall over her head to lean closer to her. "As I told you before, we can cut the time in half if we shower together. If I promise to stick to just getting a shower, everything should be fine. C'mon, Scarlett, we're wasting time." He stepped closer, reached past her and turned on the shower.

"Luke, I mean it, Toby will be here—"

He turned to catch the hem of her T-shirt and pull it over her head.

"Luke—" Her muffled protest stopped as he pulled the shirt away and unbuttoned his shirt to pull it off.

"Skin out of those clothes, sweetie. Let's hurry it up. I don't want Toby finding me in here with you." Luke stripped as he talked and stepped into the shower, turning the water temperature down to try to cool himself down, because he was saying one thing, but he was feeling another. Scarlett was naked, gorgeous, sexy and enticing. He was instantly aroused, ready to make love and wanting her.

"Don't you dare touch me," she admonished. Her hazel eyes flashed fire, and he knew he'd better shower fast and dress, but it would be the worst kind of torture. Scarlett just made him want to pull her into his arms and kiss her from head to toe.

"I'm hurrying," he said in a husky voice, "but we're coming back here to do this again later and do it right."

He washed, stepped out, dried and started dressing, watching her intently. She was breathtaking, and he was rock hard with desire. He needed to dress and get away from her and cool down fast, because he knew Toby McKittrick well enough to know he was protective of Scarlett and unhappy with Luke from his earlier years.

Reluctantly, Luke walked outside to wait for Scarlett. Images of her in the shower tormented him, and he promised himself he would coax her into showering with him again. He kicked a rock with the toe of his boot. He might not be with Scarlett much again after Toby picked up the sick calf.

"I'm ready," she said, coming outside and joining him. They walked back to the barn, and she knelt to check the calf over. Her jeans tightened across her trim, sexy butt, and once again he wanted her in his bed.

"I'll get our things packed up," he said, stepping into the next stall and gathering her things to get them stowed first. It took only minutes because they hadn't brought much. He closed the stall and carried their things to his pickup to place them in the back.

He heard a motor and saw dust stirred by an approaching car that was hidden by trees. "Your brother's coming up the road," he told Scarlett. "Our things are in my pickup, and we better get our stories straight."

"I slept with the calf. You slept—"

"Next stall. Stay as close to the truth as we can." He left to meet Toby.

Toby was big and tough, a great guy and they

had been friends until Luke left for college and abandoned Scarlett. His relationship with Toby haad been cold since that time. Since that time Toby hadn't wanted him around his sister and Luke couldn't blame him.

Toby parked beside Luke's pickup, walked around the back of it and paused a second to look at it. He picked up Scarlett's things and carried them back to put them in his pickup.

He returned. "Scarlett's inside with a calf, isn't she?" Toby asked as he approached Luke.

"Good morning to you. Thanks for coming, and, yes, she is. She has saved my horses and some of the cattle, and she's kept this little calf alive."

Toby stepped closer. "Weston, I don't give a damn that you're on *Forbes*'s list or what you've done in Silicon Valley. If you hurt Scarlett again, the way you did before, I promise you Royal will have another missing person's case on its hands. You stay away from my sister. You broke her heart."

"I've never meant to hurt your sister," he said, knowing Toby was just a protective brother. He waved his hand and glanced toward the wreckage that had been his home. "Look at the house and the ranch and see the results of the family I come from. I don't think you want me to propose to her. Not then, not now."

"No, I don't. I want you to get the hell out of Texas and away from her." Toby brushed past him, and Luke stepped aside. Toby looked back. "You come from bad blood, bad people. You hurt my sister badly before. Stay the hell away from her."

Luke watched him disappear into the barn. He didn't blame Toby for tearing into him and still respected and liked the guy. When he'd said goodbye to Scarlett when they were high school kids, he'd done the right thing, and, contrary to what she'd thought at the time, it had been for her own good.

Toby had nothing to worry about where he was concerned. His sister wouldn't want a serious relationship with Luke ever again because of the family he came from. Toby just said it—Luke had bad blood—and that point would be driven home once Toby got a good look at some of the disaster Luke's dad had caused at the Double U. Luke knew for certain that what he had accomplished in Silicon Valley wouldn't ever matter to any McKittrick. At one time, his dad had one of the finest ranches in the area, but Scarlett knew all about his parents' drinking and the results, and wouldn't ever want to tie her life to his. All she had to do was to compare his family to her family.

Luke turned to go into the barn, and Toby looked up as he approached. "Can I help get him into the pickup?" Luke asked.

"Yes, you can," Scarlett said quickly, probably cutting off Toby telling Luke to go to hell again. She began giving directions.

He knew Toby didn't want his help, but with Scarlett directing and both of them working together, they had the calf lifted into the back of Toby's pickup in seconds, with a minimum of jostling to the calf.

"Scarlett, I put your things in my pickup," Toby said. "I told them I was bringing you and the calf to the vet hospital, and they're ready for you. Thanks for your help, Weston."

"Glad to. Thanks, Scarlett. I know you'll save him."

"The hospital will," she said. "Take care of the mama."

Before he could answer, Toby started the ignition and drove off. Luke went to his pickup and got out his phone to make the calls he planned for the day. He felt a loss with Scarlett gone, and he knew that was ridiculous. Scarlett wasn't really any part of his life. The sooner he got that through his thick head, the better. He looked at the list before him and tried to get Scarlett out of his thoughts.

Will was one of the first calls he wanted to make, but as he started to dial, he received a text and saw it was the PI, Cole Sullivan. What had happened to cause Cole Sullivan to text him so early in the morning?

Five

He read Cole's text and saw that the PI wanted to meet with him, but not at his hotel. Cole suggested a private room in the Cattleman's Club at 9:00 a.m. Luke sent a text back that he would be there.

About fifteen minutes before the designated meeting time, Luke walked into the Cattleman's Club. It brought back memories of eating there with his dad, who had been a member. Later, when he was home visiting his dad, he joined. By then he was out of college and working in Silicon Valley and had started West-Tech.

He parked and headed toward the front door of the large dark stone-and-wood rambling building. New rooms had been added on through the years, but it still retained some of the rooms built in 1910.

Sunshine spilled over the tall slate roof. Inside, the high ceilings left room for hunting trophies and historical artifacts that adorned the paneled walls.

He went to one of the private meeting rooms, and in minutes Cole stepped inside and closed the door. "Thanks for coming on short notice. Meeting here seems better because, if anyone is following either of us, there's no assurance we're here to see each other. You might watch to see if you're followed."

"I will, but I go see all sorts of people in Royal. I don't think Rich will have any interest in me."

"He may be a thousand miles from Texas, but it pays to be careful. No one has found Jason Phillips yet." Cole placed a briefcase on the table, opened it to reveal papers, tablets and envelopes. He waved his hand.

"I have all this for you to sort through. Some of it, Sheriff Battle has gotten and let me copy. Some of it, I've found. The Club has been cooperative and given us some information. Actually, the big banks here have cooperated, too. They always want to catch anyone who has taken as much as a nickel from the bank. They don't give up."

Luke smiled. "Probably not good for business to let anyone get away with theft."

"This is all for you—it's copies, but this holds

information that hopefully you can use in your new programs and come up with something."

"Good deal," Luke said, moving the papers, receipts and folders from Cole's briefcase to his own.

"That's it. If you want to leave, I'll go have a cup of coffee and stick around. Or vice versa. I just don't want to walk out of here with you."

"Nope. I can sit right here and start looking at this stuff, and you can go."

"Okay. Thanks. Good luck with it. We need to nail the bastard because one man may be dead and Will was lucky he survived."

"Thanks, Cole. We can get a locker here, share the combination and you can just put info in it, and I can get it out,. And then we don't have to be here even close to the same time."

"Fine. I'll go now and get the locker, text you the combination."

"Can't beat that."

Luke shook hands with him, and Cole left. Luke put everything away and left to go back to his hotel, where he put the briefcase in the safe.

He had an appointment with the builder again and left for that.

Midmorning he saw he had a text from Scarlett telling him the calf was doing better. He smiled, thinking about this amazing woman and her way with animals. She was doing what she did best, caring for animals, being mother to little Carl. Luke always felt he was doing what he did best by working in Silicon Valley and devoting his efforts to electronics. However, now that he was in Royal, he didn't feel the urgency to get back to California that he had expected to feel.

Maybe it was just because he was needed here to straighten out the mess made by his dad. Once he got the ranch up and running and bills paid, saw his dad, helped Will get some proof about Rich Lowell, then he would probably feel that itch to get home to California. But right now, he wanted to see Scarlett. He sent her a text inviting her to dinner. She had turned him down before, and she would probably turn him down again, but maybe she would accept.

Thirty minutes later when he heard a slight ping that indicated he had an answer, he picked up his phone. She'd accepted this time. His pulse jumped, and the whole day looked better. It was foolish to feel this way. He couldn't ever mean anything serious to her or be a permanent part of her life, but she was going to have dinner with him, and he wanted it to be as special as possible.

Luke left, stepping outside to text details to her. In minutes he got a brief answer back from her that made him smile. She would be ready at five today, and she should get home by noon tomorrow. Her mother would keep Carl.

Luke's heart thudded with anticipation. She would be with him tonight. He started making arrangements, finished up his appointments, then went back to his hotel suite to get ready for their evening. He had a limo driver in his employ who was also a pilot and had flown out the day after Luke's arrival. Luke couldn't wait to see Scarlett. They'd been apart only hours, but it had been way too long. Scarlett was special. She always had been, and that hadn't changed.

Scarlett changed clothes four times before she decided on a simple, sleeveless red dress. It had a straight skirt, a belted middle and a scoop neck. Excitement made her eager for the evening. She would be with Luke, and he would see to it that they had a good time. She wanted this night with him. She'd had too many empty nights, too many tears shed long ago over him. This was a special moment, a night to share with him and she wanted it.

She opened a drawer to look at jewelry, which she didn't wear often. She touched a gold bracelet and picked it up to look at it. Luke had given it to her after they had made love the first time.

She couldn't ever get rid of it. She never wore

it—she had worn it when they dated, but once he left her, she dropped it into a bottom drawer and didn't see it often for a long time. Now it looked sort of like a kid bracelet. She just had never wanted to part with it.

When she was ready, she stepped into high-heeled red pumps. Her hair was short, easy to run a comb through. She checked her reflection in the mirror one last time and then went to find Carl and her mother. Joyce had just finished feeding him.

"Mom, I would take him, but he has little bits of food on him."

"Don't pick him up. He could easily spit up. You look pretty, Scarlett."

"Thanks, Mom. Now stop worrying. Luke is taking me to dinner to repay me for taking care of his animals and saving this little calf."

"I just don't want him to hurt you again."

"I'm not sixteen, and I'm not going to get hurt," she said, hoping she could live up to that promise.

She looked at her baby and he smiled, his dimple showing, and she had to laugh. She leaned closer to him. "You're trying to get me to come close and then you'll get part of your dinner on my dress. You'll probably think it's prettier that way." He laughed, and she did, too. "You are sneaky, Carl McKittrick," she cooed, and they both laughed again. "Mom, isn't he adorable? I think he is," she said, without waiting for her mother's answer.

"He has the best disposition of any baby I've ever seen. I thought you did, but he's even jollier than you were. Scarlett, are you sure you want to go to Dallas with Luke tonight?"

"I'll be careful. Stop fretting, Mom."

"Never," her mom said with a beleaguered sigh. "Oh...you have mail that came this afternoon. I didn't get out to the box until late. It's in the dining room. You have something from Luke."

"He paid his bill, but he said he sent something extra and to use it to help the strays I take in," she said, hurrying to get the mail. She moved slowly as she returned. "Mom, he said he sent this because he knows I help strays and all that. He said just to put it in my business however it will help," Scarlett said, staring at the check in her hand in Luke's bold scrawl.

"What's wrong with it? You sound worried," her mother said.

Scarlett stared at the check and then looked up at her mom. "I can't take this. He said use it to help animals. I still can't do it."

"Why not?" Joyce asked, frowning. She crossed the room to look at the check. "My heavens! That's half a million dollars, Scarlett. You could build a whole second facility with that."

"I could do all sorts of things, including buy TV spots where I could show the dogs that are up for adoption. Half a million, Mom. I could do so many helpful things for the rescue animals with that much money."

"No, I don't think you should. You don't want to owe Luke Weston anything. Half a *million*. Scarlett, he wants you. He's trying to buy you."

She shook her head. "Luke knows me well enough to know that if he gave me five million, I wouldn't feel obligated. It's a gift. He can afford it, and I can use it to help stray and injured animals. I can add on so we can take in more homeless animals. I have to give this one some thought."

"Just don't let his money get you carried away."

She looked at her mother. "Mom, don't worry about it. Whatever I do, the money won't make one bit of difference about how I view Luke. He broke my heart once. It won't happen again, especially not because Carl will be involved. I'm not going to do anything to let Luke hurt Carl."

"If you weren't my daughter, I wouldn't believe that. But you *are* my daughter, and I know you, and I think you mean every word you just said."

"Honestly, he may just be that grateful. You can't imagine how pitiful his horses and some of the cattle were. They were just hours away from dying, Mom. If I hadn't been there, he would have had to put them down. You've lived on this ranch long enough to know what that's like and how much it hurts when it's just one animal. When it is a lot of livestock, it's excruciating. I saved him a lot of money, too." She smiled. "Not half a million, mind you. But, in any event, I'll think about this. I can save so many animals if I cash this check. I won't have this chance again."

"Just as long as it doesn't come with strings."

"Luke knows me better than that."

"Your brother will blow his lid."

Scarlett laughed. "Yes, he will. Toby will be suspicious of Luke's motives. I'm sure of that."

"Your brother is just protective."

"I know it. He's a good brother. A little over-bearing sometimes, but good. Just wait until that cutie daughter of his grows up and starts dating. I feel sorry for the boys that go home with her."

Her mother smiled. "His daughter may have enough of Toby in her that she'll be a match for her dad."

Scarlett laughed as the doorbell rang. "There's Luke. Bring Carl and come say hello. I don't dare carry Carl in there in this dress."

Her mother wiped Carl's face, unbuckled him and picked him up to follow Scarlett toward the front door. As Scarlett went to the door, Joyce carried Carl into the living room.

When Scarlett opened the door, her heart skipped a beat as she looked up at Luke. He wore a navy suit, a white dress shirt with gold cuff links, a navy tie and black boots. He had on a white Stetson, and he took her breath away. She didn't think she had ever seen a man look as handsome as Luke did at that moment.

"Hi. Come in and say hello to Mom and Carl."

"Hi, yourself. You look gorgeous," he said and she smiled.

"Thank you." She led him into the big living room where Joyce was holding Carl and turned to face them, smiling at Luke.

"Hello, Luke."

"Hi, Mrs. McKittrick." He walked closer. "Hi, Carl." Carl gave him another dimpled grin. "He is one friendly kid."

"He gets smiles all day," Scarlett said, "so he's friendly in return. He's a happy baby. Don't stand too close. He just had dinner, and he might have some food stored in those little fat cheeks. Food that he could blow out all over you. That would give him a laugh."

Luke grinned. "Thanks for the warning. He looks delightfully harmless. So he has a sneaky side."

"He just thinks it's funny." She leaned over to kiss Carl's cheek and moved away quickly. "Bye-

bye, sweetie. Mom, I have my phone and I'll keep in touch."

"Both of you have a nice evening," Joyce said politely.

Scarlett knew her mother didn't want her to go out with Luke and hadn't forgiven him for the hurt he caused when she was a teenager. But Scarlett always wondered if Luke had wanted her to drop out of school at sixteen, marry him and go off to California with him, if her mother wouldn't have fought that to a bitter end. She had a feeling that her mother and her brother both would have been adamantly against her marrying Luke. Scarlett shoved aside the speculation on the past. It hadn't played out that way, and her mother and her brother were both still angry with Luke. Either way, he had lost their friendship.

Luke took her arm, and they walked to the waiting limo.

When they were settled in the back seat of the limo, she smiled at Luke. "Thank you for your so very generous check to me for my vet services."

"I'm really grateful for all you've done, Scarlett."

"Your check goes way beyond what I did."

"Not to my way of thinking. No other vet would have given me the time and attention that night that you did, and you know it. No one else would have worked straight through the night. No other vet would have saved as many animals as you did. Not only that, I can afford what I paid you, and you can use it to save a whole bunch more mutts." He sighed heavily. "Too bad you didn't come along in time to save old Mutt. I did love that dog, and I should have taken him with me to California. There are a lot of things I should have done."

"You need to stop blaming yourself for all your dad's shortcomings, Luke. You had no idea."

"You're right. I need to leave that all in the past and just fix things as fast as I can."

"You've really stepped up, Luke." She met his gaze. "And, yes, I'll use your generous check to help the rescue animals and get some up-to-date equipment for my clinic, and I'll give part of the money to the Royal Veterinary Hospital."

"Save your money there. I've already sent them a check because of my calf."

"You get what you want in life now, don't you?" she said, smiling at him.

He looked at her without smiling. "Not really. There are some things all the money in the world won't buy," he answered, his blue-green gaze holding her mesmerized. Was he talking about her? She drew a deep breath and told herself that was ridiculous. She didn't mean anything to Luke beyond a quick romp in the hay. He had proven that a long time ago.

"I suppose, Luke."

"You're lucky, Scarlett, to have little Carl. I never thought I'd feel that way about a baby, but he's a cute little kid and I'll bet he brings you and your family all kinds of joy."

"Yes, he does. Toby and Naomi's daughter is a little doll, as well. It's fun to have the little kids in the family. You'll have a family someday, Luke," she said, thinking of that half million.

He shook his head and looked out the window. "I don't think so. I never want a marriage like my folks had. That's strike one. I have bad genes. That's strike two. I don't want to settle down. Strike three. Three strikes, and you're out," he said, and she heard the bitter note in his voice.

She took his hand. "Luke, you don't have bad genes," she whispered. She shouldn't be holding his hand. She shouldn't be caught up in sympathy for a man who was handsome, sexy and one of the richest men in the country. Why did it hurt to hear him say he had bad genes and he didn't want to marry? Luke had walked out on her years earlier, and he hadn't really changed in all the time between. He liked making love. He was lusty, sexy and energetic. But his heart was so locked away, she wasn't certain he could find it.

Scarlett swallowed a lump in her throat. She shouldn't care, but no matter how hard she tried, she *did* care. So very much. And now, she was going with him to Dallas for a night—a night that would bind her heart to him more than ever. She was on the verge of falling in love with him all over again, despite knowing how badly she was going to get hurt again What was important was keeping Luke away from Carl. She intended to keep her baby from being hurt. She didn't want Luke in her life again because if he was, Carl would love him and get hurt, too, when Luke went back to California.

She should tell him to turn the limo around and go back to her safe, quiet life that she had before he came back to Royal and melted her with fiery kisses, taking her to paradise with his lovemaking. She was going to spend the next twenty-or-so hours with him and fall all the way in love with him. And in the end she would end up burned even worse than the last time.

She had read about him, seen the pictures of the celebrities he was involved with in California. They could give him babies that were his own bloodline, and they were gorgeous women with dazzling careers. If she thought he would ever fall in love with her, she had lost her grip on reality.

"You're quiet, Scarlett," he said, taking her hand

in his. "A penny for your thoughts. That's a silly old saying."

"Just thinking about the evening."

"I've been thinking about it all day—since the shower this morning. We can do that over tonight or in the morning and do it right," he said in a husky voice.

But if, by some miracle, he fell in love with her and asked her to marry him, she would have to say no. She couldn't give him babies. She couldn't have his children. A man like Luke would want babies that had his blood in their veins. She felt certain of that, in spite of his spiel about bad genes. He couldn't really think that he had bad blood after all the gizmos he had patented and the fortune he had made from his inventions, the company he had built and the success he had. He was smart, strong, healthy, and he definitely had good genes.

She couldn't trust him to stay. She couldn't let Carl think of him as dad only to have him walk away. She looked out the window of the limo and felt as if she were riding straight into a disaster of the heart.

"You are way too solemn. Something's worrying you."

She smiled. "Sorry. Sometimes I worry about my patients after I leave them. I need to stop stressing about them, but sometimes it's impossible."

As the limo slowed, she glanced out to see a plane waiting on the Royal airport runway. In minutes they were aboard, and she gazed out the window as they taxied down the runway to take off.

"Your limo driver is up front with the pilot?"

"There are two of them. Jake also has a pilot's license, so he's up there, where he can fly if necessary. I don't like to take chances." He flashed a grin. "You ought to come out and see me, Scarlett. See where I live and let me show you around. California has everything your heart could ever desire. I'm partial to my part of it."

Amused, she smiled back at him. "I can't ever get far from my vet practice."

"Sure you can. If you don't have someone now who can take over when you're gone, you need to get somebody."

"Maybe someday, Luke," she said, doubting if she ever would.

In Dallas they were met by another waiting limo and another driver who worked for Luke. He had whatever he wanted, when he wanted it. And witnessing it up close made her realize how she would never fit in his grandiose world with her dogs and vet business, with little Carl and a far simpler life. She would take tonight, and maybe another night or two, but he would go back to Silicon Valley before long and would never look back. She needed to face what was ahead and not have any illusions.

In no time, he opened the door to his penthouse suite and held it for her to enter.

"Luke, this is gorgeous," she said, looking at a large, elegant living area with mirrors, oil paintings, huge bouquets of fresh flowers, statues and comfortable fruitwood furniture. The lighting was soft, and he pressed a switch for music. A table was set, and Luke lit two candles. "I've ordered dinner, and I let them know at the airport we had landed, so they should be here with our—"

The bell rang and Luke turned. "There's dinner," he said, opening the door and ushering in two waiters who wheeled a cart with covered dishes.

While they put dinner on the table, Scarlett walked to the floor-to-ceiling glass window and gazed beyond the balcony at the twinkling lights of Dallas that spread for miles in all directions. As they uncovered steaming dishes, enticing aromas of hot bread, coffee, thick steaks filled the room. Soon, the waiters were gone.

When Luke dimmed the lights, she glanced around to see him shed his jacket and tie and unbutton the top button of his shirt. As he crossed the room to her, her heart drummed, and she couldn't catch her breath. She forgot the view and the dinner. All she could see was the handsome man approaching her, the man she loved. The man who was never going to fall in love with her. At least she could face the true situation this time and wasn't in a dream world, as she had been at sixteen.

"You're all I can think about. I've wanted this moment since we stepped into the shower together this morning. You're beautiful, Scarlett. I can't tell you how you excite me." He leaned closer, wrapping his arms around her and kissing away any reply she had.

She closed her eyes and clung to him, her heart pounding while she kissed him as if it were the last kiss between them. In every way possible, she wanted to make love to him, to kiss, caress and arouse him to the point that he wouldn't be able to forget her and walk away easily. All that about bad genes—she knew he didn't have bad genes, and he had to be smart enough to know it, too. He just didn't want to be tied down.

"Scarlett, I want you. I thought about you all day today and couldn't wait for this moment. I can't wait. Dinner can."

She kissed him, stopping his conversation, relishing his strong arms holding her tightly against his hard body. His arousal pressed against her. He was ready to love, kissing her with a desperation as if tonight were their last night together. At any point in time, it could be her last night with Luke. She intended to make the most of her moments with him.

Leaning away slightly, her hands slipped between them to unbutton his shirt and push it away. It dropped to the floor. She ran her hands across his muscled chest, tangling her fingers in the scattering of chest hairs across the center of his chest.

Eagerness made her fingers shake. She wanted all barriers between them removed. Wiggling out of his embrace, she stepped back and watched him as she began to remove her clothing. She heard his sharp intake of breath when she reached behind her and pulled the zipper down the back of her dress, turning her back to him as she shrugged out of it, shimmying slightly so it fell off her shoulders and dropped just below her waist, resting on her hips. She held it and watching him over her shoulder. She slipped it down over her bottom and then let it pool around her ankles. When she stepped out of it, she turned to face him. She still wore a scrap of lacy bikini and a matching bra, and her red high heels.

While he watched her, she walked a few steps closer. As she did, he stripped away the rest of his clothes.

He wrapped his arms around her, crushing her

against his chest, leaning over her. "Damn, you're beautiful, and I want you."

She rubbed against him and wound one long leg around him. He caught her leg instantly and held it, caressing her from her knee to her bottom, letting his fingers slide over her intimately. She gasped and arched her back.

"I can't wait, love," he whispered as he let her stand while he got a condom and put it on. Drawing her to him, he kissed her while he picked her up and lowered her onto his thick manhood, easing into her.

She whimpered with pleasure and need, moving on him, locking her limbs around him while she put her arms around his neck. She wanted him, needed him to be part of her life. He was driving her wild, teasing her, a tempting torment as he held her on his thick erection.

He eased slowly out of her, lifting her off and then entering her again while she gasped and clung to him. "I want you," she whispered fiercely, desire overwhelming her. And then he began to pump, and she moved with him, holding him tightly and kissing him. Lights burst behind her closed eyes. Her pulse drummed in her ears. Bracing himself, he held her with one arm while his other hand toyed with her bottom.

Her climax burst and she moved frantically,

crying out and then sinking on his shoulder as he pounded in her, reaching his own climax. She didn't know how much time passed as they gulped for breath, trying to calm their racing heartbeats. She slowly lowered her legs, and he withdrew. Then he pulled her into his embrace, and they stood holding each other. He ran his hand lightly up and down her back, over her bottom and up to caress her nape.

"I've wanted you naked in my arms since we left the shower," he said. "I couldn't keep my mind on anything else for thinking about you all day," he said.

She turned her head to gaze up at him. "I'm glad. I want you to want me. I've always wanted you, Luke. I hope I'm in your dreams at night and in your thoughts during the day." She trailed her fingers over his chest and ran her tongue along his throat, his ear, back to his shoulder, letting her fingers glide suggestively down his hip.

Still holding her tightly, he scooped her up and carried her to the shower. "We can shower and eat in bed if you want."

She pursed her lips. "We're not taking any food to bed. It would end up spilled, and we'd be making love in the gravy."

He grinned. "Scarlett, oh, baby, how I like being with you," he whispered and drew her close against him to hug her. He turned the water on, got it warm and began to run his hands over her wet body.

"Here goes dinner," she said, doing the same to him, gliding her hands over his hard muscles, bulging biceps and flat belly. When he ran his hands between her legs and began to toy with her, stroking her, his other hand caressing her breast, she gasped and closed her eyes, clinging to him as she moved her hips.

"You can't be ready again."

"I've got two hands," he whispered. "I can take you to a climax with my fingers," he said, rubbing her intimately.

She writhed against him as he started another storm of desire. He turned her, sliding his thick cock between her legs, holding her close as he rubbed against her, and she cried out, all the while using her hands to try to excite him as much as possible. And then she was lost in sensation as tension grew and she felt as if she would burst with need.

"See what you do to me," he said, his words husky, claiming her lips with his before he picked her up and thrust his hard rod inside her. She gasped and cried out, holding him tightly, wrapping her legs around him and moving on him until an orgasm burst through her and release came.

He shuddered with his climax, pumping in her, emitting a throaty growl as he shifted his hips, and then he finally slowed and held her tightly.

"I think that might have been able to go in Ripley's list. I didn't think that was possible so soon after I reached a climax."

"You don't know your own possibilities," she whispered, kissing his shoulder.

"One of us has been working more than the other of us," he said. "Give me a break."

She smiled. "You're saying you don't want me to kiss you, or caress you, or rub against you—"

"For the next ten minutes—no, fifteen minutes—Scarlett. Then you can do whatever you want to do."

"Whatever I want to do?" she said, smiling mischievously at him. She turned to let the water run over her, washing and then stepping out to grab a huge, fluffy bath towel. When she began to dry, Luke took the towel from her and dried her, rubbing her lightly, watching her as he ever so slowly dried first one breast and then the other.

"You're beautiful," he whispered, leaning forward, bending to run his tongue over her nipple. Sensations streaked from his hot, wet tongue making circles.

He walked behind her and began to dry her back, starting at her shoulders and slowly moving down. She turned to stand on tiptoe and kiss him briefly and then leaned back.

"Now I get to dry you." She ran the towel over his strong body, pausing to touch his hip. "I remember this scar—bull riding when you were eighteen."

"I was lucky I didn't break any bones. My bull riding career was short. Very short."

He tossed the towel away and grinned down her. "So far we've had a good start to the evening. Want to have a glass of wine? Beer? Eat dinner?"

"I'm ready for some dinner, except I'm not eating naked. I want clothes, and let's go sit on the balcony and look at the lights.

"Whatever the pretty lady wants, the lady gets. The one plus about wearing clothes to dinner is that I will look forward to taking them off of you *after* dinner."

She smiled at him. "Give me a few minutes on the balcony to enjoy the city lights."

He caught her hand and brushed a kiss on her knuckles as they walked back to get their clothes and dress again. "This is good, Scarlett."

"I think it is," she answered. She paused. "I'm ready to eat now. Let's get our plates filled and sit on the balcony."

"Sounds like a deal." Dressed again, Luke

draped his arm casually across her shoulders. "Scarlett, it's good to be with you."

Her heart missed a beat. "I'm glad," she answered truthfully. "It feels very good to be with you like this, as well." Was he just being polite? Was it euphoria after making love? She knew better than to count on his remark having any deeper meaning, but hope took root anyhow.

"It's beautiful up here, Luke," she murmured a few minutes later, looking out at the sparkling city lights as Dallas spread out in all directions. Luke had poured wine and they had helped themselves from a spread with lobster, salmon, steak and creamed pheasant. She was more captivated by the view and the handsome man across from her than her dinner.

"Absolutely breathtaking," he said in a deep, raspy voice that caught her attention and made her turn to face him. He smiled a slow, hungry smile that held a promise of kisses to follow. Her heart thudded.

"*You're* breathtaking, Scarlett. I like being with you, and I'm glad you're here tonight."

"This is magical, Luke. I'll always remember tonight."

They sat quietly, Luke eating while she had a few bites of lobster with melted butter. "I'm glad you're keeping the Double U ranch. You'll have a fine ranch again."

"I'll have a fine new house. I'm going to have at least three houses—one for me when I come back. One for someone I'll hire to run the ranch and be responsible for it, and a third for a guest house. There might be more, but that's a start."

She wondered how much he would come back to Royal. "That's a good start, Luke."

I just have to hire the right people. Either that or come home and do it myself, and I'm not ready to turn rancher."

"You were good at it when you lived here."

"California is my home. You should come see me, Scarlett."

She smiled at him. "I wonder if I'd love it the way you do," she answered, certain she would never see his Silicon Valley home.

"I've put it off long enough and my anger over the ranch has cooled slightly... I need to go visit my dad. Would you go with me? That'll keep me from yelling at him."

"You won't yell at him. Especially now, because it sounds as if he's very ill."

"I think he is. It's sad."

"I'll go with you if I can. Just let me know when."

"Sure." They sat quietly eating. She wasn't very hungry and she enjoyed the view.

"Let's go inside," he said, standing and taking her hand. They walked into the living room. He blew out the candles and turned to face her.

"Come here," he said. Before she had taken three steps, he picked her up to carry her to the bedroom, where he stood her on her feet. He framed her face with his hands and leaned closer to kiss her. As her arms went around his neck, he wrapped his arms around her.

Scarlett's heartbeat raced. She kissed Luke, knowing with full certainty that she loved him, wondering if he even had a glimmer of a notion that she felt so deeply for him. It wouldn't matter. She wasn't the woman for him, and she never would be. Luke would have his happy, rich, wonderful California life, and she was glad. He belonged there, and she belonged here in Texas with her baby, her mother and all her family. She was needed here. Her job was important and she had saved more than a few animals. Carl was happy and she didn't want that to change. It was just unfortunate for her that they could never have anything beyond what they had tonight—a fun time making love, good company and that's all.

She held him tightly and kissed him, wanting him, wishing she could just keep holding him.

It wasn't possible, and she had to take what she could and live with the beautiful memories. And she didn't want to worry her mother or get Toby all riled up and angry with Luke. She hoped this time around she could keep her feelings from all of them. But could she really hide what she felt for Luke?

Sunshine spilled into the room and across the bed. It was 8:00 the following morning, and they'd slept in each other's arms between the times they made love throughout the night. Scarlett had to get back to Royal. As sweet as Carl was and as capable as her mother was, she didn't want to leave her mother to deal with her son for too long. She told Luke she needed to get home, and he agreed because he was getting information from Will about the missing Texas Cattleman's Club money.

"Okay, Scarlett, the jet's fueled and ready to take us home."

"When we get there, I'd love for you to come in and see Mom and Carl. Mom will want to hear about the Double U∆ and Carl will just want some attention. I bought him a toy downstairs in the gift shop."

"I should get him one, too. Come help me because I have no idea what's safe to give him or what he would like or what is appropriate for his age." He grimaced. "Scarlett, I know absolutely nothing about babies."

"You did fine with him. He liked you, and you made him happy. You don't need to get him anything. He's happy whether or not he has a toy. And he does have plenty. I just can't resist taking him something."

"I suspect he likes everyone he meets and he's happy all the time."

She smiled. "That's true. You did quite well with him, and I'm sure he'll be happy to see you again."

They started to go to the door, and Luke caught her arm, pulling gently. Surprised, she turned to look at him.

"I don't want to leave yet."

"Luke, we can't hole up here—"

"One more kiss," he whispered and slipped his arms around her to draw her closer as he leaned forward and placed his mouth on hers. The minute his lips touched hers, her arguments vanished. She dropped her things and put her arms around him, holding him tightly, feeling each time they were going to part that it was probably the last time she would see him before he left for California.

When he ran his hand over her breast and then reached for the zipper to her dress, she caught his hand and stepped away.

"You're headed for another hour in bed, and we can't. Let's go, Luke. We both have things to do and places to be."

For a moment she thought he was going to argue with her, but then he nodded and reached around her to open the door. As they walked out, she felt as if she was walking out of his life for the final time. Would she feel that way each time she left him?

Six

Luke returned to the Bellamy to his suite. He'd had his computer set up where he could work. Cole was getting information to him about the stolen money with dates and what little records on withdrawals the PI had unearthed. Luke worked at night, going to the Double U in the day to see what progress they were making and to go over plans for the new ranch house.

On Monday, Luke asked the architect for a copy of the plans so he could review them back in Royal. That afternoon, he called Scarlett and told her he'd like her to look at the plans for the new ranch house and see if she had any suggestions. "I need a woman's perspective."

She laughed. "Sure. Come have dinner with us.

Mom is cooking her chicken and dumplings, and they're good."

"I remember and they are good, and you don't have to ask me twice. What can I bring for Carl?"

"Like I said the other day, you don't need to bring him anything. He'll be happy to see you. Just smile at him."

Luke laughed. "It's easy to smile at him because that's all he does. Does he ever cry?"

"Of course, he cries. He can get grumpy when he's tired. But most of the time, he's happy."

"He gets that from being around you."

"I hope so. I try to be happy around him. So far, he's a sweetie."

"I never knew a little kid could be fun, but yours is," Luke said.

"It's good that you like him," she said, but her voice had a wistful quality, and he wondered if he had said the wrong thing.

That night when the doorbell rang, Scarlett opened it to welcome Luke. She took a deep breath as her heartbeat sped up. He wore a white shirt, navy slacks and his black boots. Taking off his black Stetson when he entered the house, he filled the room with his masculine presence, and she couldn't help noting that he looked more handsome each time she saw him.

"You look great," he said softly, his gaze sweeping over her and making her tingle. They wouldn't be alone until maybe late this evening before he went home. She just wanted to walk into his arms and kiss him.

"Thanks," she said, wondering how many outfits she had pulled out before she decided on her blue sleeveless dress and sandals. "Come into the kitchen. Mom's cooking and Carl is playing with his toys."

"I brought the house plans. I'll leave them with you—these are copies. Look at them when you can, and we'll get together to discuss them. I want your input."

"Sure," she said, thinking with a pang that she would never live in this house she was going to help him plan. Would he ever marry, or was he just going to avoid marriage because of his parents' disastrous marriage?

Her mother came from the kitchen to greet Luke. She wore a bright red apron over her gray slacks and white blouse. Her honey-blond hair grazed her shoulders, and her vivid blue eyes sparkled with warmth. Scarlett knew how angry she had been with Luke in the past, but that was gone tonight and she was her usual friendly self. "It's good to have you here with us, Luke. It seems like old times."

"It smells wonderful in here. Thanks for having me for dinner. The Bellamy food is good, but I remember yours, and there's no comparison."

She laughed. "I remember you used to like the chicken and dumplings."

"Yes, I did, and I imagine that I still do." Scarlett walked to Carl, who sat in a little bouncy chair. Scarlett picked him up and handed him to Luke.

"Hi, Carl," he said, smiling.

Carl smiled back and patted Luke with a chubby little hand. "Ahh, those dimpled smiles of his. Let's look at the toys." Luke glanced at Joyce. "Mrs. McKittrick, can I help you in any way?"

"No, thanks. We'll be ready to eat in about half an hour. I'm going to check on the dumplings. I'll join you two again in a few minutes."

"Sure, Mom. When you're ready, I'll help get dinner on the table." She turned to Luke, who was playing with Carl, swinging one of his toys back and forth.

"What would you like to drink? Beer, red wine, white wine, margarita, old fashioned, whatever. Mom has a well-stocked bar."

"I'll just have a glass of water, thank you. Scarlett, I've been drinking beer since I was about sixteen or sooner. My folks didn't care. Now when I look at alcohol, I just think about the ranch and Dad, and I don't want a drop." He exhaled roughly.

"I know that will pass, but that's the way I feel right now. I just keep seeing the sick livestock and the dead carcasses."

"I can understand. That was a shock."

"Does your brother know I'm here tonight?"

She shook her head. "No, I don't think Mom said anything about it."

"I'm glad. Keep peace in the family. Your mom's cooking is fabulous. This is going to be a real treat. This and maybe a few other things," he said, winking at her and she felt her cheeks grow warm and knew she blushed.

During dinner Luke entertained them and he also fit in and Scarlett was sorry Toby couldn't accept Luke.

At one point Luke smiled at her mother. "Dinner is delicious and this is great. I feel at home here," he said, looking at Scarlett and she was startled that he felt totally welcome and at home during dinner. Her mother had a way of making company feel part of the family.

After dinner, Luke said he would clear and for Joyce to join Scarlett and Carl and put her feet up. After a polite argument, which Scarlett ruled, she and her mother cleaned the kitchen, leaving Luke with Carl.

When Joyce and Scarlett joined him, all of them had to smile at Carl's antics.

Scarlett smiled with the others, but she felt a pang. It was wonderful to have Luke with them, but soon he would go back to California, and she really didn't expect to ever be with him like this again. Luke would marry some wealthy woman, and his life would move on.

At one point, Luke picked up Carl and held him on his lap, making faces and funny noises at the baby, and when Carl laughed, all of them laughed. Scarlett got her phone and took a picture of Luke and Carl, both laughing up a storm. She couldn't resist—she shifted and took a picture of Luke.

"A baby's laughter is contagious," Scarlett said, loving having Luke play with Carl, yet wanting to avoid times like this too often where Carl would get attached to Luke.

"He sounds so damn happy," Luke said. "Whoops. I better watch my language around him. At least he won't copy me tonight."

Finally, Joyce picked him up. "I'll take him up to bed. Kiss Mommy goodnight, Carl," she said, handing him to Scarlett, who hugged him and kissed his cheek.

"Mrs. McKittrick, that was a wonderful dinner. Thanks for including me. You have a cute grandchild."

"Thanks, Luke. He keeps me young. I have so

much fun with him. And as he grows, he just gets to be more fun."

"Well, he's the first baby I've ever been around. He's set the bar pretty high."

"He's special. Come back and see us, Luke," she said. "You're always welcome."

"Thank you. That means a lot," he replied. Scarlett knew from her mother's tone of voice that she had meant what she said to Luke, which had surprised her. And she thought Luke was also sincere in his answer. His answer didn't surprise her, but she intended to ask her mother about her remark.

He smiled as Joyce left with Carl in her arms.

"She sounds as if she means that," he said to Scarlett.

"She does or she wouldn't say it, believe me. I think you mended some fences with her tonight. You said and did all the right things, and you took a second helping of her chicken and dumplings, which she loves to see someone do."

"You've got a great family, Scarlett. I've always thought that. Is your mom coming back?"

"No. She'll read to Carl and then rock him, and when he finally goes to sleep, she'll go to bed to read. We've seen the last of her tonight. Want to go to my place? It's next to this house."

"Sure. Carl sleeps here, and you sleep there?"

She shook her head. "Nope. I still have my suite

here, and Carl's nursery is here because Mom keeps him so much of the time while I work. I just stay over here since I got Carl. I don't mind. There's no husband—just Carl and me—so we might as well stay here. And, besides, Mom is here and she loves taking care of him."

Luke put his arm around Scarlett's shoulders. "Scarlett, I hope you say, 'Thank you, God,' every day in your prayers for your family. You are so blessed to have them. My dad can be mean as a snake."

"Believe me, I do." She gazed up at him. "Your dad wasn't that mean when you were growing up, was he?"

"Not to me. He and Mom fought like a mountain lion and a rattlesnake. They had big fights—verbal, not physical—but then they'd drink themselves into not caring, and life was bearable. Actually, I just got out of the house as often as I could—worked on the ranch, hung out with the cowboys, went into Royal to see my friends. Later, went out with you."

"You didn't complain."

"It was just a fact of life and when I was away from it, I didn't want to talk about it."

As they talked, Scarlett took him next door to her house. "I've had this all redone," she said. "I used to have my office downstairs and I lived upstairs. I had my clinic and everything out here, but later, I built in Royal and then changed this from an office downstairs turning all of it into a house for me. I didn't think about becoming a mom then. I don't spend much time over here now," she admitted, stepping inside and switching on one light. "Come look around." She led him into a living room that was rustic with framed paintings of horses and ranch scenes on the walls.

Luke turned her to face him. "It feels good, Scarlett. Being with you just feels so damn good. Tonight was just like I'd come home, only my home was never as filled with love as this one is," he said and pulled her to him to kiss her.

Her heart thudded and she wrapped her arms around his neck as their lips met. She pressed against him, desire sweeping over her. "Luke," she whispered and then kissed him again, tightening her hold on him. He shifted, his hands moving to the buttons on her dress to unfasten it.

"Do you have a bedroom in this place?" he rasped against her lips, kissing her between each word.

"Oh, yes," she answered breathlessly. "I'd hoped we'd end up here. The bed is ready."

Scarlett pushed against him, turning so she could walk backwards while they kissed. He continued to kiss her as he followed her from the living room to her bedroom.

She had unbuttoned his shirt and pushed it off him, pulling it out of his slacks to toss it away. While she peeled away more of his clothes, he began to remove hers. She stepped back from him to unfasten her bra and take it off, watching him as he yanked off briefs. Her breath caught in her throat and her pulse pounded. He looked magnificent with his muscled body, his broad shoulders and trim waist, his narrow hips. Just looking at him made her throb and want to reach for him, to feel his hard body pressed against hers.

"You look like one of the California stars," she whispered, running her hands over his shoulders, his biceps and his chest.

"You're the one who's gorgeous, Scarlett. You take my breath away and keep me awake at night. You're beautiful. Your body is stunning, and the sight of your legs can have me ready for love in seconds."

His hard erection sure was ready, and she slid her fingers over the smooth tip, leaning down to run her mouth over him, curling her tongue around him and stroking his rod while she toyed with him between his legs. She peeled off her panties and reached out again to caress his erection, leaning close to run her tongue over him again, and then turning to rub her bottom slowly against him.

He reached around her, fondling her breasts, circling her nipples with his thumbs so lightly that she gasped with pleasure.

With a groan deep in his throat, he wound his fingers in her hair as she knelt to kiss and fondle him.

She heard his sharp intake of breath and then, in seconds, he swept her up into his arms, carrying her to bed, where he stretched out and pulled her on top of him. His body was marvelous, masculine and strong, and hard-muscled, his arousal big and erect. She wanted him with all her heart, wanted to hold him and not let go, but that was impossible and she knew it.

She was astride him as he positioned her over his hard cock and then pulled her down to enter her, thrusting inside, filling her and beginning to move.

Closing her eyes, she cried out, feeling him hold her hips as he moved with her, pumping into her, each thrust and withdrawal heightening the tension that gripped her. She rode him hard and fast until release burst and she cried out in ecstasy, falling over him and gasping for breath.

"I can't move," she whispered.

"You're fabulous," he said, trailing his hands

over her back and down over her bottom. "So beautiful, so sexy. This is paradise," he whispered. One hand stroked her bottom while the other fondled her breast. "Scarlett, I'd like to touch you all night long."

"You can't. We have to go back. I sleep in the room next to Carl, and I get up with him at night so Mom doesn't have to. He doesn't always wake up, but I can't stay out here tonight."

"Okay, I'll get up and go home soon, but let's take one more hour, maybe one more round before I go."

She smiled as she sprawled over him, her fingers running through the hair on his chest. "I might be talked into that," she purred.

"If I have to talk you into it—"

"Surely you can think of something persuasive," she teased. "But not yet. For right now, just hold me against your heart and let me hold you and pretend you're not going to leave me."

"It's good to be together. It feels right, doesn't it?" His voice was a lazy drawl as if he might be on the verge of sleep. She suspected it might just be euphoria, him rambling without really thinking about what he was saying. She wished he meant it, but she was certain he didn't. In any case, it felt right to *her*. She loved him and had loved him since she was fifteen years old. Sadness gripped her. She wasn't the woman for Luke, and she knew it. He didn't think he was the man for her, but he was being ridiculous. He would never be like his parents. Luke had too much drive, self-discipline, control. He didn't have bad genes. She couldn't argue much, however, because she knew she could never be his wife. He needed a woman who could have his babies. She thought of precious little Carl. How lucky she had been to get him. She couldn't get a more wonderful child.

She kissed Luke. If only—"if onlys" were impossible. She had to take life like it really was, but she was thankful for what she had, thankful for Luke in her arms tonight, that they could have memories. So thankful for little Carl, the joy of her life. Thankful for Toby, Naomi, her little niece, Ava, her precious Mom. They had a wonderful family, and when she was with Luke and he talked about his family, she knew how lucky she was. It was a good thing Luke wouldn't be around a lot because they would never marry, but Carl would love Luke so easily. Luke was great with Carl. She could spend a bit of time with him while he was in Royal, but it was just as well that he would go back to California soon.

She showered light kisses on Luke's throat, shoulders, chest and then snuggled against him. She loved him and there was no way to keep from loving him. She would get hurt again, but this was worth some hurt.

"Some terrible things brought you home to Texas, but we have this, and, to me, this is marvelous," she whispered. "I know it can't last, but, Luke, it's so good. In your arms is the best place to be."

"At least I can help right some of the terrible things, and you've already helped me make it right. You saved so much of my livestock."

"The little calf is getting stronger each day. I hope you took care of the mama."

"I did," he assured her. "There are cowboys out there now taking care of the animals. I don't even need to go every day, but I have been. When I go back to the hotel, I'll go back to work. I hope we can nail Rich on the money. Cole is bringing me all sorts of info. That, my love, is absolutely for your ears only."

"So your antifraud software is working?"

"We haven't found anything so far, but we're just getting started and putting in the info we have. I think we'll find something eventually."

Running his fingers lightly over her breasts, he sighed. "Ah, Scarlett, this is even better than my memories of us. I didn't know that was possible."

"I quite agree," she said, caressing him, thinking she could never get enough of touching him, kissing him, being with him. Too soon he would be gone forever. At the thought, she tightened her arms around him and held him close.

It was two in the morning when he stepped out of bed. "I think I better go back to my hotel now. I don't want to impose on your mom's hospitality. Her cooking improves with age. She's a fabulous cook, while you, my darling, are a fabulous sexpot. You're wonderful in bed."

"Stop that, Luke Weston!"

He laughed. "You love me to tell you how sexy you are, and you know it. Scarlett, you have to be the sexiest woman in all of Texas."

"Now, that is such a stretch that it's absurd. You better stop your exaggerations about me being sexy, or I'll stop doing all those sexy things to you that you love to have done—like this," she said, stroking him.

"You convinced me," he said, drawing a deep breath. "You'll be in town tomorrow. Call me when you can have lunch, and I'll buy you a burger at the Royal Diner, and it'll be like old times. Afterward, let's go up to my hotel, and let me introduce you to my bedroom and my shower."

She grinned. "I might take you up on that offer, although a bedroom and a shower? Nothing new there."

"I might have some new tricks to show you in the bedroom."

"Now that does catch my interest." They both laughed and kissed, and she held him, looking up at him and smiling. "We can have fun still, Luke. We used to have a lot of fun together."

He gazed at her and he suddenly looked solemn. "We sure did, Scarlett."

"I don't know about old times, but I'll take you up on that lunch. I'll call you." She dressed as he did, but she watched him and drew a deep breath. She wished she could go right back to bed and spend the whole day making love with him. He was the most handsome man she knew, and she still had the best time with him of anyone ever.

As she reached for the door to leave, he caught her wrist. Surprised, she turned, and when she saw his face, her breath caught. His arm went around her waist, and he drew her to him, leaning down to kiss her. He covered her mouth possessively, kissing her thoroughly, with hot, fiery passion. Finally, he stepped back. His blue-green eyes were dark and stormy as he gazed intently at her.

"I better go, Scarlett," he said gruffly, turning to hurry out into the darkness. Outside lights burned and in seconds he was on the path back to the main house, where she caught up to walk beside him.

"It's been fun, Luke."

"It's been perfect. I'll see you tomorrow at lunch." At his pickup, he turned, hugging her tightly, and bent down to give her one last mind-blowing kiss. When he released her and climbed into his pickup, she watched, dazed, her lips tingling while she wished once again that he wouldn't ever leave her.

She stood there until his pickup's red taillights faded from sight. She was hopelessly in love with him, but he hadn't given her any indication that he wanted her for keeps. She sighed. For Carl's sake, it was for the best. She might end up with a broken heart, but at least her son's heart was safe. Still, how much hurt was she going to have when Luke left Texas?

Later that morning, Luke got a text from Will to meet him at the Texas Cattleman's Club. Once again, Luke went to a private room, where this time he found Will waiting.

"Thanks for coming. News has come back from the handwriting analysis of the note Megan Phillips received, the note that her brother was supposed to have written. Jason Phillips has been excluded by a margin of 99.9% of being the note's author. Consequently, Richard Lowell has not been excluded as the person responsible for Jason's disappearance. In fact, now he's the prime suspect."

"Wow. We're beginning to get proof. Oh, damn. It's great you're alive, but I'm sorry because it isn't looking good for Jason."

"No. We won't have a positive answer until we get the DNA report on the bone fragments in the ashes in the urn. Ashes that were supposed to have been mine. If you can find some ties to the stolen money and Rich, we will have absolute proof that he's responsible."

Luke scoffed. "He may be far, far away on some island, enjoying his ill-gotten gains and planning his next crime."

"We'll get him. We have to. I wanted to tell you in person. Also, even though no one knows where Richard is, we're all beginning to learn what he's capable of doing, so be careful."

"I will. I'll let you know what I find about the money."

"I want proof so he can't ever wiggle out of facing the consequences for what he did. Especially if those are Jason's ashes, and right now it's not looking good. Poor little Savannah. She's only six years old, and I know she misses her daddy terribly. At least she has her aunt Megan and her uncle Aaron." He shook his head. "I'd better take off, but let's keep in touch."

Luke followed his friend to the door. "You can count on it, Will."

As soon as Will departed, Luke went back to his computer to work on following Richard's money trail.

The next day, with more information from Cole, Luke was able to trace some of the money taken from the Texas Cattleman's Club back to the accounts Richard Lowell had used when he'd been pretending to be Will. He sent a text to Will to inform him to let him know that now they had proof.

In the afternoon Luke drove to the Double U to meet with his new builder. Scarlett had looked at the house plans with him Tuesday night, and he'd had another dinner at her house. Why did it feel so right to be with her, to be at her family home? And it amazed him how much fun he had with her little baby. Every time he was there, it also made him wish things were different, that his family legacy wasn't one of destruction.

It made him feel better to go to the Double U now because the animals were looking a degree better. When he drove up where the house once stood, the land had been cleared. Since the house was in such terrible shape, he was relieved he didn't have to keep looking at the wreckage.

On Thursday, when he drove back out to the Double U, Reuben Lindner had hired cowboys.

Again, Luke was amazed how much better the animals looked each time he drove to the ranch. He felt another stab of gratitude to Scarlett and admiration for her dedication and ability. He thought of the moments of passion, of holding her in his arms after making love, of her sexy, soft, beautiful body that set him on fire. If only he didn't come from the family he had. There was no way he could tie his life to hers. Scarlett was absolutely off limits for him forever.

He didn't know why he was even thinking about marriage. He would go back to Silicon Valley, and everyone in this town, including Scarlett, would all fade from his life once again. He had asked her to go with him to see his dad, something he dreaded, but felt it was his duty to do. He had gifts to take—chocolates, a basket of fruit, a new shirt, two books he thought his dad would like. He wondered how his dad was because he couldn't count on what he said on the phone.

The following morning, Luke held Scarlett's arm lightly as they walked into the assisted-living facility. People sat in the lounge in groups, some playing cards, others just talking or watching TV. Luke stepped to the desk to sign in, and then they headed to his father's apartment.

Scarlett went with him as they rode the elevator

to the second floor, and they walked down a long hall before Luke stopped and knocked on a door.

"I haven't seen your dad since your graduation," Scarlett confided.

"Your mom doesn't look that different since I graduated. I suspect my dad is going to look very different because of the liver disease. I'm going to have to tell him about putting everything in my name."

"He should be relieved that you saved the ranch," Scarlett said.

"Knowing my dad, he won't view it that way. He always wanted control, even when he was the reason he lost control."

Even though it had been two years since he'd seen his dad, Luke wasn't prepared for the man he faced when the door opened. His father's gray hair had thinned, and Bruce Weston looked shorter. Luke guessed his dad had lost sixty or seventy pounds from the way his clothes hung on him. Instead of the ruddy complexion he always had from working outside, his skin was wrinkled, yellowed and pale. Shocked, Luke had another stab of guilt for not coming home more often and keeping up with things.

"Dad?" Luke said, reaching out to shake his father's hand.

"So you really did come home."

"There wasn't much home left to come back to, Dad. You remember Scarlett McKittrick."

"Joyce McKittrick's girl. You're all grown up now, Scarlett. I heard you're a vet. Imagine that, a woman vet. Y'all come in and have a seat. Sorry the place is not cleaned up for you."

"I brought you some things," Luke said, setting them on a table.

"I don't suppose a bottle of whiskey is in there?"

"No, Dad, there's not," Luke said, knowing his dad had not been kidding. They walked into an apartment that had papers on the sofa and dishes on tables. "Dad, don't they clean your apartment for you?"

"Yes, someone comes. I tell them to leave things alone. I don't want them messin' with my stuff."

"I think you should let them clean. You'll be in a swamp before long if you don't."

"My friend, Charlie, his girl works for the city and saw the papers. I heard from Charlie that you put the Double U in your name. You took my ranch away from me."

Luke drew a deep breath, wondering when his dad had gotten so quarrelsome. "The sheriff's office was going to auction the ranch, and we wouldn't have owned it any longer. It's been the Westons' land since the early days of Texas settlement. I thought it should stay in the family, and, yes, it's in my name now. Which means I'll take care of the bills for the ranch and your bills here. You won't have to worry about any of it."

"Well, I can't stop you from taking it away from me. I'm not surprised. You've gone out to California and become a rich, successful hotshot. You're going to live life your way, and you've got the money and the means to take the ranch from me. I'll get out of here someday, but I guess I won't go home to the ranch. Or are you going to let me go back to the Double U?"

"If you get well and move out of here, you know you can go back to the ranch," Luke said, hanging on to his temper because his dad was old, ill and not thinking clearly. And sober, he was mean and bitter now. With some drinks, he became jolly.

"Do you feel better? I talked to Dr. Gaines, and he said you don't want the rehab nurse to help you get a little exercise."

"That quack. What I'd like is for you to bring me one bottle of whiskey. One bottle wouldn't hurt, and it would be the one and only bottle in almost a whole year. Now, that is long enough for anyone to go without a drink. If you want to be nice to your dad, come back by while you're here and bring me a bottle."

"I don't think that's good for you, Dad. You don't want to end up back in the hospital."

"Indeed, I don't. Get a bottle and bring it by. That isn't going to put me back in the hospital."

Bruce turned to look at Scarlett. "You've joined the Texas Cattleman's Club, haven't you, missy?"

"Yes, sir, I did. They've included women for some time now."

"Oh, I know they have. They have a nursery for screaming kids and a playground. The minute the females got in, they took it over, which I figured they would. The Club has been going to hell since they let women like you into the club, greedy single mothers, too hard and unwomanly to keep a man."

"Dad, that's uncalled for and absolutely unfitting for Scarlett, who has spent hours saving Double U livestock that you didn't take care of and left to starve to death. I think we've paid our visit, and we're not doing any good here, so we'll say goodbye," Luke said, standing, trying to hang on to his temper.

"Let's go, Scarlett." He took her hand and led her toward the door. "We'll let ourselves out. You just keep your seat."

"Luke, you come back by and bring me a bottle of whiskey. That's the least you can do when you've got the ranch now."

"Sorry, Dad. Not until Dr. Gaines tells me to bring you a bottle." He opened the door, and they stepped out, then he closed the door behind him. A moment later, he heard something smash against the door and fall. Luke shook his head.

"The last few years, he'd get meaner when he was sober, but that happened so seldom when I was around that I didn't give it much thought. He wasn't ever *this* mean. He must have run the men that worked for him off the place. Sorry, Scarlett, that he tore into you. He doesn't know what he's talking about."

She reached up and gently cupped his jaw. "I'm sorry for you. He doesn't bother me. I haven't seen him in years and probably won't see him again. The active members of the Texas Cattleman's Club don't seem to share his views. There are two or three who still object to women belonging, but otherwise everyone seems okay with it."

"I'm definitely okay with you belonging," he said and smiled, but his smile faded. "Seriously, you see what I mean about bad genes running in my family."

"Luke, you don't have bad genes, and you're not like your dad, and you're not an alcoholic. I haven't seen you drink anything. You don't inherit being mean, either."

"I have the same blood in my veins, and it worries me. And despite what you think, I know deep down that I've been a terrible son to him. I neglected him and the Double U and failed to do what I should have done."

She blew out an exasperated breath. "Luke, I will keep telling you this until it gets through your thick skull! You *can't* blame yourself for what your dad did, and besides he told you over and over again that everything was all right."

"I hear you, Scarlett, I do. It's just a bitter pill to swallow." He took her hand again, and they headed back down the hallway to the elevator. "He had no business to call you greedy and talk about single moms ruining things. Too hard and unwomanly— that doesn't fit you and never will. I shouldn't have taken you with me to see him."

"Stop worrying about it. It doesn't mean anything to me. You got here in time to save the ranch and you own it now and you're getting it back in shape. That's all that matters to me."

He sighed as they stepped into the elevator and headed back down to the lobby. "Ahh, Scarlett, you're so forgiving."

"About some things."

"Why do I think that remark is directed at me?"

"No. You're wrestling with a guilty conscience, so things just strike you that way." She squeezed his hand. "Let's go to my house and talk to Mom and see Carl. My little boy will cheer you up."

"I'll bet he will," Luke said, smiling as they left

the elevator, headed to the exit and then climbed into the back of the waiting limo. "Before we do that, let's have a stop at my suite in Royal. That will cheer me beyond measure," he whispered, brushing a light kiss on her lips and then looking into her big, hazel eyes. "Okay?"

"Of course," she whispered back, sliding her arm around his neck. He picked up the phone to tell Jake to take them to the hotel in Royal and later they would go to Scarlett's ranch.

He turned to wrap his arms around her to kiss her. She *would* cheer him up. So would going to the McKittrick ranch and seeing little Carl. Why did being with Scarlett seem so right? He was missing work in Silicon Valley, missing making megadeals that he had loved to do. He felt drawn to this Texas town and to hanging with Scarlett and her baby. Was it the near loss of his family legacy that had upended his world and changed his priorities? Or something else far more personal? He sighed, once again reminding himself that he couldn't start dreaming of a future with Scarlett and her little baby because he might wreck both their lives. All he had to do was look at his dad and what his dad had done. And was still doing. He had been terrible to Scarlett.

He had bad genes, and Scarlett and her eternal optimism couldn't convince him differently. She saw the world through rose-colored glasses, and she didn't see the reality in his life at all. Not even after his dad criticized her so much.

"Luke, you're quiet, and I know what's worrying you. You'll never ever be like your father, and it is just absurd for you to worry you will."

He gave her shoulders a slight squeeze as he forced a smile. "I hope you're right," he said, but he wasn't feeling particularly optimistic right now.

As soon as they were in his suite, he drew her into his arms. "I don't know much right now but I *do* know I want you in my arms now more than I could want anything else on this earth."

He meant what he said, and, as he kissed her, he wondered how important she was becoming to him? Was he falling in love? He'd better not because it wouldn't have a happy ending. It was just so good to be with her. So fantastic to make love to her. She sent him up in flames, and he knew he would never forget these nights with her. Before he could walk away from the ranch and leave Royal behind once and for all, he wanted to make more memories with Scarlett, memories he would never forget.

He had the life he wanted in Silicon Valley. Constant deals, chances to develop new ideas, new electronic gadgetry, money beyond his wildest dreams and his pick of beautiful women. It was a fun, carefree world with no strings attached, so why did that sound empty and no longer hold the same attraction and pull that it once had?

"Scarlett, have dinner with me in Dallas. I'll get you home early in the morning."

She knew Luke was unhappy, worried he would end up like his dad and incredibly hurt to find him in such a bad shape. She also knew he was angry with his father for what he said to her, but she wasn't disturbed by the ramblings of an old, sick and bitter man who was probably suffering from a guilty conscience for his misdeeds as much as from his booze consumption.

She nodded, agreeing to go with Luke because time was running out for them, and she also might be able to cheer him up. "Thanks, Luke. I will. Mom's good about keeping Carl. I'll send her a text."

The minute they closed the door on his hotel suite in Dallas, Luke turned to draw her into his arms and kiss her. He paused, raising his head to look into her eyes. "You make the world better for me, Scarlett. When I'm with you, my problems seem to fall away and all seems right with the world."

Luke carried Scarlett to his bedroom, where he stood her on her feet by the bed and kissed her again. His fingers unfastened her buttons and soon all clothes were gone, and he held her in his arms in bed while he caressed and kissed her.

She trailed her fingers over him while he did the same for her. He made love with a sense of desperation, taking her fast and hard. Afterward, he turned on his side, cradling her close, wanting to hold her and never let go.

"You've saved me again, Scarlett. I needed you tonight."

"Luke, I'm sorry. I know it hurt today to see your dad that way."

Luke tenderly combed her hair away from her face with his fingers. "You're good, my love. So good. When you're in my arms, it's the best feeling in the world. That's as good as it gets."

"Ahh, if only you really meant that," she said softly.

He held her, running his hands over her, finding solace and comfort in just having her close. Even so, he still couldn't get the visit with his father out of his thoughts. Seeing his dad just convinced him more than ever that their paradise couldn't last. If he truly was his father's son, he had no business promising Scarlett and little Carl forever.

He cuddled Scarlett against his side while he ran his finger up and down her slender arm. Her skin was smooth and warm. "Scarlett, this is a dream come true, but I don't want to mess up your life."

"You're not going to mess up my life. I like having you in it—or haven't you noticed? Why do you think I'm here in your arms?"

"We're good together in a physical way, but I'm not the man for you. I don't have to tell you why. You were aghast at the condition of the Double U. You can't just shrug that off. That blood runs in my veins, too. You've seen my dad. Is that going to be me years from now?"

"No, you'll never be like him." She brushed a kiss on Luke's cheek. "Maybe we weren't ever meant to be, Luke. It isn't just you. I'm not the woman for you. You should have children who have your blood in their veins, your talents. I can't give the man in my life children who are blood kin. That's what it should be for someone exceptional like you."

"That is just ridiculous. You have an adorable son. You shouldn't ever worry. You couldn't have a cuter little baby. You clearly can adopt a baby, and the blood in my veins could get a kid in a hell of a lot of trouble. Bad genes, remember?"

"You have good genes, but you leave. Your life is California, not Texas. I can't risk loving and saying goodbye again. I'm a mom now and I don't want my baby to love you and then you walk out. I have to think about Carl."

He took a deep breath while he frowned. "We just weren't meant to be. I don't plan to stay in Texas. I'm a workaholic, and no woman likes that."

She smiled and got a twinkle in her hazel eyes that made his breath catch. She ran her finger over his chest. "The right woman might get you to come home at night and quit work early in the evening," she said in a sultry voice.

"You think?" he asked, his voice getting deeper as he slipped his hand behind her head and pulled her to him to kiss her. He rolled her over and moved on top of her, keeping the bulk of his weight off her.

Gazing up at him, she wrapped her arms around his neck. "You don't have bad genes. You have wicked, fun genes," she whispered. "And ooh, la, la, what a body." She pulled his head down to kiss him.

Luke's heart pounded and he was hard again, wanting her. Scarlett was unlike any other woman he'd ever had. He'd been with some breathtaking women who were sexy, enticing and eager, but no one could excite him as quickly or to the extent Scarlett did. She had freckles, an adorable pixie cut, a gorgeous body with lush curves and long, long legs—every man's fantasy woman come true. But even more importantly, she had her own view of life, and his money didn't mean beans to her. Neither did his job or the power he had to do things. Scarlett was very much her own person, and he could warn her about bad genes until the sun fell out of the sky, but she would draw her own conclusions and stick by them.

"You're a puzzle in a lot of ways," he whispered, trailing kisses over her throat and ear. "You're not impressed by things that impress other people. You put a high priority on helping others and animals, but you don't have a qualm about telling me to go to hell when I annoy you."

She looked into his eyes. "Luke, you worry too much. And you'll never figure me out." She kissed away his answer, and he forgot their conversation as he deepened the kiss and ran his hands over her tempting body. He rolled on his side, taking her with him and thrusting his leg between hers to move them apart so he could caress and fondle her. He heard her gasp and felt her arch against his hand as he stroked her. He wanted her in his bed, in his arms for the entire weekend if he could talk her into it.

On Saturday, Scarlett sat in her office in her veterinary clinic in Royal right off the downtown area. Luke had brought her to work that morning from his hotel, and he was going to see Will and Cole Sullivan. He had asked her to have lunch with him afterward. They were together constantly now, and when he left Royal and went back to Silicon Valley, she was going to miss him terribly. She knew he would go back without her and without even thinking about asking her to go with him. He understood that she had a life here and would never leave it. Just as she knew he had a life in Silicon Valley and was certain he would never want to leave it, either. They just weren't meant to be as they had agreed. He thought he had bad genes, and she knew she couldn't trust him to stay.

If he got the Double U running efficiently, would he even come back to Royal again? He and his dad were obviously not compatible. His dad was being taken care of. The ranch should run smoothly. There was nothing to bring Luke back, and she suspected, the next goodbye would be permanent. Tears pricked her eyelids. She'd loved him all her life, and the thought of never seeing him again hurt deep inside, but she couldn't turn back time or change the future.

Her intercom buzzed, and the receptionist spoke up. "Scarlett, there's a man to see you. He said he knows the way and wants to see you in your office. His name is Tanner Dupree."

Seven

Surprised, her first inclination was to say she was unavailable and refuse to see him. Instead, she said to send Tanner back to her office because she felt obligated to hear him out since they had a history together. She was shocked her ex had returned.

A few moments later, he knocked lightly and entered. "Good morning. I should have sent a text or called, but I didn't want you to say no."

"I wouldn't say no, and I'm surprised. Please have a seat." Nodding, he sat in a leather chair on the other side of her desk facing her.

"You look great, Scarlett."

"Thank you. So do you, Tanner," she said and meant it. He had thick brown hair that had a slight wave and thickly lashed pale brown eyes, and was several inches over six feet tall. As usual, he was well dressed in a dark brown suit and tan tie. Although he was undeniably handsome, he had never made her heart race the way Luke did. She sighed despite herself. Luke, with his blue-green eyes, dark blond hair and mouth that she loved, could make her heart pound even when she was angry with him and she didn't want to feel anything.

Tanner looked at the picture of Carl on her desk and picked it up. "This is a new picture. It's not your brother's baby, is it?"

"No, Tanner. That's my son, Carl. Remember, I started adoption proceedings because you wanted me to have a baby. There was a lot of pressure from your family. Well, after you left, a newborn became available, so I adopted him."

"I'll be damned. You're a mother," Tanner said. "I'm shocked you went through the adoption alone. They contacted me and I had no interest in adopting at that point. I assumed you didn't either. I hope in the future you can at least try fertility treatments to conceive a biological child. I can overlook that you went ahead without me," he said, staring intently at the picture of Carl.

"They needed a home for this baby, so when they called I said yes. End of story."

"I'll tell my family. That will make them very happy. I've heard of women who adopt suddenly getting pregnant without fertility treatments. Scarlett, I regret leaving and now, with you having a baby, this is better than I expected."

She listened to him without even really hearing what he was saying, and knew with full certainty she would never marry him. The truth was, she had never really been in love with him the way she was with Luke. If she ever needed proof she loved Luke, here it was. She felt nothing for Tanner even though she had almost become his wife.

"Tanner, thank you."

He looked startled. "For what?"

"For walking out. We weren't really in love, and I realize that now."

"Scarlett, how can you say that? We were almost married. I just made a terrible mistake. I had pressure from my parents because they wanted an heir and you couldn't get pregnant, but now you're a mother and you can see a doctor about getting pregnant."

"Tanner, I—"

He held up a hand. "No, please, Scarlett, let me finish. You see, I've got it all worked out. I went to Chicago and thought I'd go back into sports, being an agent, but I've given up being a sports agent. I'm going into the family oil business, and I'll take over for my dad when he's ready to retire. After you and I marry, we can live in Dallas where I'll work, or we can reside in Royal where your clinic is. It's your call."

"Tanner, can you hear me?" she said, trying to be patient. "We're through. You walked out, and that was that. We're not getting back together. Thank you, but no thanks. We're finished forever."

"Give me one more chance."

"There's just no point, Tanner," she said. "I'm not in love with you, and I know it. I don't think we were ever really in love. You wouldn't have walked out if you'd truly been in love with me."

"Is there another man in your life?"

"No, there's not," she said because she knew any day now Luke would go back to Silicon Valley and she might not see him for years, if ever.

"I've heard your old boyfriend, Luke Weston, is back in town and you two have been together a lot."

"Yes, we have," she admitted. "His father left the family ranch in shambles, with the livestock starving and dying. Luke needed my help."

"Are you two a couple?"

"Not at all. I saved some of his livestock, and he was grateful. Mom has had him out for dinner because he was a family friend, but he has never asked me to commit to him. He has his Silicon Valley life, and I have my vet life in Royal, Texas. We have no future plans. Luke is a long ways from getting married, and so am I…and definitely not to each other."

"I'm glad to hear that. So I don't have any big competition?"

"Tanner, have you not heard a word I've said? You and I are *not* in love. I don't know why you left. I don't know why you're back. I have my baby, Carl, and he's adorable. I don't want to marry, and even if I did, it would not be to you."

"I can't believe you're saying that. Please, let me take you to dinner. I'd like to see your son. My parents will be so happy to hear that you have a baby. A baby we both could have had. I'm so sorry I walked out. I got scared about such a big commitment. I have huge regrets."

"It worked out for the best. Find the right person. Someone you want to spend the rest of your life with. Someone you love who loves you back, with her whole heart and soul."

His eyes turned hard and angry. "Are you sure this isn't because of Luke Weston? You were in love with him once."

"No, Tanner, Luke isn't the reason why. You and I are finished."

"At least just go to dinner with me and tell me what you've been doing. Tell me about this little boy. You surely will give me that much, won't you?"

She smiled politely and shook her head. "I'm

sorry, but the answer is no. You made your choices. I'm making mine. Going to dinner won't change anything."

"I made a terrible mistake."

"Actually, Tanner, the way it all worked out, I have my little boy now, so, in my eyes, what you did was never a mistake.

She walked around her desk and toward the door, hoping he get the hint. She breathed a sigh of relief when he followed her. "I've missed you," he said.

She shook her head. "My life has changed a lot, and we can't go back and undo our pasts."

"We did have fun, Scarlett."

"Yes, we did, but it's over now." She stepped into the hall, and, when he followed, she stepped back into her doorway. "You know the way out."

Tanner clamped his jaw closed, nodded tersely and strode away. She knew he was angry, but he had made his choices earlier and now he was living with the results. He had just walked out on her when they were ready for the wedding and then disappeared without a word. Looking back, she realized that Toby hadn't been nearly as angry over Tanner practically leaving her stranded at the altar as he had been with Luke when he broke up with her all those years ago. For the first time it

dawned on her that Toby might have been happy
to see Tanner go out of her life.

As she walked back to her desk, she thought of
the few times Toby had been around Tanner, and
he had been cool and not quite his usual friendly
self. She smiled because Toby had never said an
unkind word to her about Tanner until he bailed
on her, but now she realized Toby never had liked
him in the first place.

When she had dated Luke in high school, Toby
had liked him. This anger with Luke had come
about after Luke left for California and hurt her
so badly.

She closed the office door and crossed the room
to pick up Carl's picture. Love filled her and she
smiled. This was why Tanner had been good in her
life. Because of his insistence on a baby, she had
started the adoption procedure, and then Tanner
left and she got Carl, her own little boy. She put
the picture against her heart and hugged it lightly.

Setting the picture back on the desk, she looked
at her calendar, called her assistant and told her
she was going home for a couple of hours, something had come up. She called her mom to tell her
that she wanted to come home to get something
and she would see her shortly. She had called just
to make sure her mom and Carl would be home.

Smiling, she grabbed her purse and left through

the back to hurry to her car and head home to the ranch.

She passed the hotel where Luke was staying and thought of him naked in bed, a thought that made her draw a deep breath. At this hour he would either be poring over the information Cole Sullivan had provided, or out working on something else. He wouldn't be in bed by himself at this hour.

She couldn't wait to get home and hold Carl in her arms. Her son was the only reason she could think kindly about Tanner and be glad that he was in her life briefly. There was only one man who was the love of her life, but he wouldn't return her love, and she couldn't trust him not to break her little boy's heart.

Even so, she loved Luke Weston with every fiber of her being, and it was going to hurt even worse than before when he left.

Luke sat in the Royal Diner over coffee. He had met with Abe Ellingson yesterday afternoon, and they had pored over the house plans and everything was set. He had an appointment today with Reuben, who had already hired three men to help. Reuben had wanted Luke to come to the final interviews on the first men he hired because Reuben wanted one of them for the foreman job. He wanted the other two because they could take charge in the foreman's absence. In a few more days, everything should be moving smoothly along, but Luke hadn't felt any rush to return to California.

That shocked him because Silicon Valley had been his world for a lot of years now. It was Scarlett that held him here, and he knew it. It didn't do any good to know the reason because he couldn't do one thing about it. He was not messing up Scarlett's life and little Carl's. His visit with his dad had brought back how terrible things had been at his home when he was growing up with two drunks for parents. He was going to see to it that that never happened to him, but the best way was to stay single. He had been supremely happy with his no-strings life in Silicon Valley. Why did it seem so empty now?

"Luke Weston?" a deep voice said, and Luke glanced up to see a tall man facing him, and he recognized him from pictures.

"You're Tanner Dupree," Luke said, but he didn't stand and he didn't offer his hand.

"May I join you?"

Luke wanted to tell Tanner to go to hell and wondered if Scarlett had—or had it gone the other way? Had she been happy to see Tanner again? If Tanner was in town, he felt certain the man had already seen Scarlett.

"Sure. Have a seat. Want coffee?"

"No, thanks. I've been with Scarlett this morning. Actually, mending our relationship. I made a colossal mistake leaving her. Especially when we had started adoption proceedings. I got jittery—a wife, a baby and all." He cleared his throat. "Anyway, I've been to see Scarlett, and she showed me the picture of our baby. We're getting back together so our baby will have a mom and dad. She said there's nothing between the two of you."

"No, there's not," Luke said, suddenly hurting badly, feeling as if he had been stabbed in the gut. He thought about the hours he had spent with Scarlett. Was Tanner lying to him? He didn't know if Tanner was telling the truth—it didn't matter. He realized he loved Scarlett. Forever love with all his being even though she could never be his. He couldn't be a dad for Carl, a husband for Scarlett. He loved her with all his heart and he thought her baby was adorable.

He was losing Scarlett again—except she had never, ever really been his to lose. He realized Tanner was still talking.

"I'm taking her out tonight to celebrate. We'll have the wedding soon because all plans had already been made before. She said you were an old friend, nothing serious between you."

"No, there's not," Luke said stiffly, knowing

that was the damn truth. There wasn't anything binding between them, and there never could be. Damn his heritage. He had always known that she couldn't be his. He wasn't the man for Scarlett. He wasn't the man to be part of her family. They were the family he always wished he had as a kid. Still did, for that matter. Mrs. McKittrick would never be mean to a friend of Scarlett's, the way his dad had been to Scarlett. Toby was a good guy and a reliable one.

He couldn't even hear what Tanner was saying, but he gritted his teeth and tried to focus on him.

"Good luck, Weston, although you don't need it. I saw the *Forbes*'s list. Impressive. Congratulations."

"Thanks," Luke stated without thinking about it.

Luke didn't believe Dupree. He just wanted him to move on and out of his life.

"Goodbye, Weston."

Luke nodded and swirled his coffee. The minute Tanner was out of sight, Luke paid and left. He'd finally acknowledged that it was Scarlett keeping him here, even though he should have ended things already. But now, it had to be over. It was time for him go back to Silicon Valley.

He made arrangements to fly back to California late in the afternoon. Next, he phoned Cole and scheduled an appointment to meet with him at

1:00. Afterwards, he called Abe and Reuben and filled the two men in on his travel plans. By the time he had finished all the calls, it was time to meet with Cole. Luke missed lunch, but he didn't feel like eating anyway. While he and Cole talked in Luke's hotel room, Will joined them.

"We can tie some of the stolen money from the Texas Cattleman's Club directly to the accounts Richard Lowell used while he was assuming Will's identity," Luke said. "I have more information from Cole, and he's learning this program, so I can work from California and he'll work here. We'll coordinate with conference calls."

Cole looked up from the computer screen and ran his hand through his tangled, short, dark blond hair. "This is fantastic. It's the more recent transactions. Rich is getting a little careless, and he isn't trying to pass himself off as you now. He's got his own name on some transactions he's made."

"Thank heavens for that one. I have some other good news," Will said. His green eyes sparkled, and he had a faint smile. "At least, it was something that needed to be done and I think it's going to be good. Brent Smith, an attorney from Dallas, showed up at Aaron's house. It's official now— Aaron Phillips has been appointed guardian of Jason's daughter, Savannah. She loves her uncle Aaron. Megan has been alternating with Aaron to care for Savannah, but Megan agrees it's best to have an official guardian. Legally, it is definitely best. I'm still shocked by the terrible things Rich has done."

"Well, with the handwriting analysis, a bit of the stolen money actually traced from the Club to him, and soon we should have the DNA report on the bone fragments in the ashes, probably Jason's—there's going to be a solid case to nail this bastard," Luke said.

"Catching him can't come too soon. How soon are you leaving, Luke?"

"Late today. I've been away too long. I need to get back to work and to my business."

"Sure," Will said, offering his hand. "It's been great to have you here, and thank you for all your help. Seems sort of like old times."

"'Sort of' is right," Luke said, with a crooked grin. "No fake funerals back then."

"Hell, no. I do hope there are no more surprises like that. Go back to your golden world where everything comes up smelling like roses, to drag out an old cliché. Mrs. Hodge, our old English teacher would shudder." They both smiled, but Luke hurt and was trying to hide it.

When he was finally through and went back to the hotel to throw his things into a suitcase, all he could think about was leaving Scarlett and little

Carl. How could he get so damned attached when he'd gone into this knowing he shouldn't?

His heart was telling him to stay and fight for Scarlett because he loved her, but he thought about his bad genes, and the last thing he wanted to do was cause Scarlett to end up with a family like the one he had. Maybe after seeing his dad so sick and mean, she would understand his decision. Maybe she really was going to marry that Dupree guy.

He was going back to the life he had wanted. He'd vowed to never allow himself to be tied down. He excelled at building smartphones and software programs, not relationships. But could he return to his lush Silicon Valley life as if these past couple of weeks—the best of his life—with Scarlett and her adorable kid had never happened?

Luke threw things into his suitcase, hurrying as fast as possible. He wanted away from Texas, back to the life he had in Silicon Valley, where he wasn't torn to pieces loving a woman he couldn't have, loving a little baby he wouldn't be able to watch grow up, loving Scarlett's whole damn family because they were the family he never had.

But most of all, loving her. Scarlett was everything—gorgeous, smart, fun, sexy, kind—and he'd loved her all his life. She was the only woman he had ever truly loved. "Dammit," he muttered. Glancing at his watch, he rushed out of the room, taking the stairs two at a time and racing to his car to drive to her clinic.

"I need to see Scarlett as soon as possible," he told Tracie, her receptionist. "It's private, so I'd like to see her in her office."

Tracie smiled at him. "I'll tell her, Mr. Weston." He wanted to go on back to her office and not wait, but he tried to be patient.

"She said to come to—"

He was gone, letting the door close behind him as he rushed down the hall and into her office. "I'm leaving, Scarlett. I wanted to see you before I go."

As her big, hazel eyes widened, she stood up. She had a white medical coat over a pale blue cotton blouse and a pair of jeans, and she'd never looked more beautiful. "You're going back to Silicon Valley," she said.

"I just wanted to tell you goodbye. I don't expect to see you again for a long time. I don't think I'll be back this way."

She blinked, and all the color drained from her face. She raised her chin. "My second goodbye to you. This one is probably permanent."

Luke crossed the room and swept her into his arms to kiss her, crushing her against his chest, kissing her as if it was the last kiss of his life.

Shocked, hurting, Scarlett clung to him until he swung her up, gave her a look that made her tremble. She started to reach for him, but then he was gone, slamming her office door behind him.

Stunned, Scarlett stared at the door. That had not been the kiss of a man who wanted to tell a woman goodbye. She touched her tingling lips with her fingertips. That had been the kiss of desperate man. One would have thought he'd left to face a firing squad.

She stood blinking, trying to figure out what had just happened besides Luke saying goodbye— a goodbye that sounded permanent—and then rushing out of her office as if he were chased by demons. What was going on with him?

Her intercom buzzed, and she rushed to answer in case he was coming back. Instead, it was Tracie reminding her of an appointment. She had dog surgery, and she had to stop thinking about Luke and his kiss and focus on her patient, which she did.

For almost the next two hours, she was busy with her patient. Once the surgery was over, one of the assistants would take over for the night to check regularly on the dog and make sure everything was all right and that the dog wasn't in pain.

Scarlett glanced at a wall clock. She tried to call Luke, but his phone was turned off, and she knew he was airborne, heading back to his California life and flying out of her life, maybe forever. One question kept niggling away at her, over and over again.

Why had he been so desperate to get out of town? Luke set his own schedules, so if he hadn't really wanted to go back to California yet, he wouldn't have done so. Was he trying to get away before he broke down and proposed? She might think that, except he could get very iron-willed when he felt strongly about something, and he felt strongly that his "bad genes" would ruin not only her life, but Carl's also.

And if he really felt they had no future together, why such a frantic, possessive, final kiss that conveyed so much desire it made her knees weak and her heart race? For the first time since she was a teen, she felt that Luke loved her. That kiss had been filled with love. What upheaval had happened in his life to send him running for California, but first to come kiss her goodbye?

She ran a comb through her short hair and headed out to her car to drive home. Tanner was waiting for her in the parking lot. "You don't look as if you've been working all day. It's wonderful to see you again, Scarlett."

"Tanner, what are you doing here? This seems a waste of your time and mine."

"Not at all. Give me a chance. I know you're angry with me, but what we had at one time was good, and we planned a wedding together."

"A wedding you walked out on. You act like

that never happened. It happened. Live with the consequences. We all live with consequences."

Her cell phone rang and she saw it was Toby. "Excuse me, Tanner. This is Toby," she said and walked a few steps away, wondering what was happening.

"Is everything okay?" she asked him.

"That's why I called and what I was going to ask you. I saw Tanner today. He's back, and I just want to make sure you're all right."

She smiled. "Tanner isn't the violent type, Toby. Go play with Ava or hug Naomi. I'm fine."

"Okay. I know I'm butting in, but he was sneaky before, and I just wanted to make sure everything was all right. He said you've gotten back together."

She frowned. "He told you that?" she asked, stunned that Tanner would lie about their relationship. Who else had he told that to?

"That's what I thought. I didn't think you'd go back with him the minute he showed up again. I just wanted to make sure he wasn't up to something. He obviously wants back in your life."

"You're a very good, considerate protective brother, Toby. Thank you. I'm fine. Don't worry about me, and I'll talk to you later."

"I heard Luke went back to California, and I thought maybe that was why you went back with Tanner."

"Oh, no. I haven't gone back with him and I won't."

"Frankly, Scarlett, I'm glad. That's a crummy guy who will walk out and leave you stranded at the last minute before a big wedding. I've been angry with Luke for hurting you, but you two were teens. Luke was up front with you about everything. He didn't blindside you when he left and then come try to take you back. Okay. I'll stop being nosy big brother."

"You did good, bro. I love you for it. Thanks." She ended the call and hurried back to find Tanner still leaning against her car. "Tanner, have you been telling people today that we're getting back together?"

"It may have been premature or presumptuous, but, yes, I have, because I think we will. I want to, and if you'll give me half a chance, I think you'll want to, too."

"Listen closely. No, I don't want to—now or ever. Sorry, Tanner. Best wishes for a happy life." She unlocked her car door and pulled it open.

"Scarlett, don't go."

"There's just one man for me. I'm going to try to save a Texas cowboy from himself," she said, smiling and driving away, trying to avoid speeding.

Now she knew the reason Luke had kissed her as if life was going to end. He loved her, bad genes or not.

Maybe this time he'd be willing to stay.

Eight

The next morning, Luke walked through his Silicon Valley mansion. It was quiet, filled with all kinds of electronic conveniences. The house was mostly glass, giving spectacular views of the California countryside. It was contemporary, with large expensive modern oil paintings by famous names and unique, one-of-a-kind furniture. He had enjoyed it, felt at home in it, loved the contrast to the old-fashioned ranch home he grew up in.

He had a huge-screen television, streaming shows that he liked, a gym. Why did it seem so empty and cold since his return? He had a cook who did an excellent job, with two assistants to help in the kitchen if necessary.

Luke didn't feel like eating. He missed Scarlett. Hell, he missed Carl, he missed Royal and his friends. What had happened to him on his trip home? It wasn't as if he didn't have friends here. He called one of the women he enjoyed the most and talked about twenty minutes and ended the call without asking her out. He didn't want to go out with her. She was a beautiful blonde singer who was hitting the top of the charts and he'd had fun with her. But his mind wandered while he talked to her, and he knew he couldn't get through an evening with her.

"Scarlett," he said, talking to an empty room. "What have you done to me? What have you done to my life?" All the years growing up, he dreamed of the life he had found in Silicon Valley. Now it felt empty and not what he wanted at all. He felt alone and restless, and when it got right down to it, he missed Texas, Royal and his life there.

He groaned and stared out a window. He had been a workaholic, billionaire bachelor, but from his sterile, modern marvel of a home in Silicon Valley, his carefree, no-strings existence was beginning to feel like a whole lot of lonely. And his heart was far from free. It was very solidly in the possession of a stunning, take-no-prisoners Texas cowgirl.

Was he tossing aside a wonderful family and life because he was scared he couldn't control himself enough to avoid becoming a drunk like his father?

Luke hadn't ever stopped to think about whether he could have enough self-control, but he'd spent all his life using self-control one way or another. Why had he let his parents' addiction change and govern his life?

He sat in his silent house and then went out by his pool and sat watching a waterfall and a fountain in his pool, thinking about his future. With Scarlett as his wife and little Carl his son, he would never turn to drink. He loved them too much.

Why the hell had he thought he couldn't have enough control to avoid losing them because of drink?

He had been through college, built a company, developed a successful smartphone, developed programs. He'd had deadlines, stress, tests in college—why did he think he would just buckle and become a drunkard, dependent on booze like his dad? All his life his mom and dad had fought. Maybe that had driven them to use alcohol excessively. He didn't know, but maybe he was all wrong in assuming he would be like them. He was in his thirties and had no problem dropping alcohol altogether. He ran four miles a day. That took self-discipline. He worked out an hour a day besides the running. More self-discipline.

Had he lost Scarlett and little Carl all because of wrong assumptions about himself, unfounded fears that he had let control his life?

Could he go back in time to fight for Scarlett's love? He didn't think she was in love with Tanner. She hadn't sounded like she was.

He got out his phone and called her and didn't get an answer. He made arrangements with his pilot to fly back to Royal in the morning.

He sent Scarlett a text message, but didn't get a response.

Was he going to ask Scarlett to move to California and settle in Silicon Valley and give up her thriving vet practice? She might be willing to. Or would he like to open a West-Tech office in Dallas?

That appealed to him. He would be near Royal and friends, Scarlett would be near home and her family. She could keep her practice, while he would have the challenge of starting up another West-Tech branch in a city he loved in a state he loved while he lived with a woman and baby he loved. Damn, but he'd been blind.

He was going back to Texas to fight for her love.

He couldn't wait for morning, so he called and asked his pilot to get ready to leave at four in the afternoon.

He remembered some of his mother's jewelry that had been passed down from his grandmother and got a box out of his safe and carried it to a table to search through necklaces, lockets, bracelets. It didn't take long to find the necklace of small diamonds and a golden heart covered in larger diamonds. Scarlett didn't wear a ton of jewelry, but she did wear some.

The necklace was in a box lined with black velvet. He'd had the jewelry appraised, insured and then put in boxes. He put the others away, carrying the velvet box with him. He wanted a present for Carl, too. He went to a storage closet and rummaged through boxes until he found the one he wanted. It was a little teddy bear that sat on a shelf in his room. His grandmother had given it to him, and his mother never would let him play with it because she was afraid he would tear it up, so it was in good shape.

He took both presents and put them in gift bags, then tried to call Scarlett again but still got no answer. He didn't want to think about her with Tanner.

Luke got his travel bag to pack, when he heard the bell to the security gate. Surprised, he went to see who was at the gate. He looked at the picture on the monitor, and his heart thudded.

The two most important faces on earth were smiling out at him. Scarlett held Carl as she rang again.

"I'll open the gate. Come on in."

He raced downstairs and to the door to open it as Scarlett walked to the door. She held Carl in her arms, and she had a small, shaggy black dog on a leash. Carl held out his arms.

Luke wrapped them both in his embrace and kissed Scarlett while his heart pounded.

"I feel as if I'm dreaming," he said, looking down at her and then at Carl, who gave him a dimpled grin. "Scarlett, why are you here? You and Carl and a dog?"

"I was trying to figure out that kiss—why you rushed into my office, kissed me like it was your last hour on earth and then rushed out for California. That isn't exactly like you. While I was thinking, Toby called me to ask if I was going back to Tanner."

"Yeah, Tanner came by my office to tell me you are, but you didn't fly out here to tell me that," Luke said, looking intently at her. "Not with a baby and a dog. I didn't believe him."

"I'm glad you didn't because of course I'm not going back with him, I couldn't figure out why you rushed in to kiss me like that until I learned what Tanner had said. Your kiss was the kiss of a man who wanted to stay. A man in love."

"Thank heavens for your brother."

"You kissed me as if it might be the last kiss of

your life. To my way of thinking, that was the kiss of a man in love. Am I not right?"

"You figured that out just like that." His smile vanished.

"Yes, I did. That kiss meant you love me. I flew out here to fight for that love. I'm not sixteen and giving up when you pack and leave Texas."

"That's awesome. Tanner shocked me and when I hurt so badly, I really thought about my life. I realized I love you with all my being, a love I'll feel for the rest of our lives. When I realized that I truly love you, I also faced another truth about myself. Instead of giving you up, I can give up the notion of having bad genes because of my parents."

"Luke, thank goodness."

"I realized that I won't become a drunkard like my parents. I have self-control—enough for a lot of things, including resisting alcohol all the time. Mostly though, Tanner gave me such a jolt when he said you were getting back together—that was like having my heart ripped out. That's when I realized that I was deeply, seriously in love with you."

"Ah, Luke," she said.

"That's why I went to your office and kissed you goodbye, but flying back here, I had time to really think things through and get rid of old fears."

"Luke, I'm so glad that you've let go that idea of

being like your parents. There's one problem that's mine—I can't have your children. That problem isn't going away."

"Carl is a super baby and I love his mom with all my heart. Scarlett, if little Carl needs a sibling, we can adopt."

"You really mean that, don't you?"

"With all my heart. I'm not doing this right, but I can't wait a minute longer. Scarlett, will you marry me?"

"Yes, I will. I thought you'd never ask, so I came to California to ask you."

"I have a plane getting ready to take me back to Texas. I'm glad we didn't pass each other. I was coming back for you and Carl."

"You were coming back for me and Carl," she repeated. "You weren't going to leave me this time."

"Never, Scarlett."

He kissed her briefly. When he released her, he looked down at her and took Carl from her and set the bag she carried on the floor. "Hi, little guy. How do you like Silicon Valley? Scarlett, what is this little black dog?"

"It's a little black rescue dog. He's almost a year old, well-trained, sweet, and he's to make up for your old Mutt."

Luke laughed and shook his head. "Come inside, my darling. Are you hungry? Did you eat?"

"I'm too excited to eat, and Carl was getting sleepy, but I think that's gone now. Oh, my goodness, look at your house. Luke, we've got to get a pen for Carl or something. This is the most unchildproof house I've ever seen. Mercy. I'm not sure we can stay here. It's perfect for the dog, though. Mutt Two can stay here."

"Oh, yes, you'll stay here, right in my arms tonight and Carl can stay if I have to get someone to bring new furniture out here this afternoon. Or empty one of these rooms. Matter of fact, I'll get on it right now and get us a baby bed or whatever he can sleep in. Scarlett, I don't know much about babies."

"You'll learn," she said, still looking around.

"You're really going to marry me?" he asked and he looked at his phone.

"Yes, I am. I don't know if we'll have to see each other on weekends. I'd like to stay in Royal and keep my practice, so this may be a long-distance marriage."

He slipped his arm around her waist. "No way, my sweet. I'm ahead of you because I've been thinking about it."

"How about this," he said, wrapping his arms around her waist while Carl sat on the floor playing with a toy Scarlett had given him. "We live on my ranch and we'll have a house in Dallas, too. I'll open a West-Tech office—"

She threw her arms around his neck and hugged him. "Yes, yes, yes. You'd do that for me? I love you, Luke. I've loved you all my life."

"I love you, Scarlett, and I've loved you all my life, too."

"We have a lot of lovin' to make up for."

"That we do." He winked. "And I'll get a baby bed in the next hour."

"You can't get a baby bed in an hour."

He quirked a brow. "Wanna bet?"

"Okay. I'll bet you one two-hour session of hot sex that you can't have a baby bed bought, delivered, set up, and sheets washed, dried and ready in two hours from now."

"You're on. Watch what money can do. I'll get the sheets washed first." He made calls, and when he finished, he turned to her. "Now, I'll show you my big bedroom, which we can share, and we'll put Carl in the next adjoining room in my suite. And, by the way, you're the first woman to stay in this house. That makes you extra special."

Her eyes sparkled with happiness. "I am extra special. I'm marrying an incredibly wonderful man."

He grinned and tugged her into his arms. They heard Carl making little noises and looked around.

He sat holding his arms up, and Scarlett laughed as Luke scooped up Carl to hold him, too, as he kissed her. "We'll be a happy family, Luke," she said, certain they would be and that there would be at least one more child in their family.

Luke took the leash off the dog and pet it. The dog leaned against Luke's knee and wagged its tail. Luke looked at Scarlett. "Mutt Two. He's a good dog, Scarlett." Luke stood and walked to her to take Carl in his arms. He held Carl with one arm and put the other around Scarlett. "C'mon, Mutt Two," he called over his shoulder and looked down at Scarlett. "I love you, and I need to make up for a lot of lost time with you. I love you with all my heart."

"I've always loved you with all my heart," she said, smiling at him. "Life will be good, Luke."

"It will now," he said, smiling back at her, and her heart pounded with joy because soon she would marry the man she had always loved.

* * * * *

Don't miss a single installment of the
TEXAS CATTLEMAN'S CLUB:
THE IMPOSTOR *miniseries.*
*Will the scandal of the century lead to love for
these rich ranchers?*

THE RANCHER'S BABY *by New York Times
bestselling author Maisey Yates*
RICH RANCHER'S REDEMPTION *by
USA TODAY bestselling author Maureen Child*
A CONVENIENT TEXAS WEDDING
by Sheri WhiteFeather
EXPECTING A SCANDAL *by Joanne Rock*
REUNITED...WITH BABY *by USA TODAY
bestselling author Sara Orwig*
THE NANNY PROPOSAL *by Joss Wood*
SECRET TWINS FOR THE TEXAN
by Karen Booth
LONE STAR SECRETS *by Cat Schield*

***

*If you're on Twitter, tell us what you think of
Harlequin Desire! #harlequindesire*

SPECIAL EXCERPT FROM

⬣ HARLEQUIN®

Desire

*A year ago, lies and secrets separated tycoon
Spence Jameson from analyst Abby Rowe. Now, thrown
together again at work, they can barely keep it civil. Until
one night at a party leaves her pregnant and forces Spence
to uncover the truths they've both been hiding…*

Read on for a sneak peek at
REUNION WITH BENEFITS by HelenKay Dimon,
part of her JAMESON HEIRS series!

Spencer Jameson wasn't accustomed to being ignored.

He'd been back in Washington, DC, for three weeks. The plan was to buzz into town for just enough time to help out his oldest brother, Derrick, and then leave again.

That was what Spence did. He moved on. Too many days back in the office meant he might run into his father. But dear old Dad was not the problem this trip. No, Spence had a different target in mind today.

Abigail Rowe, the woman currently pretending he didn't exist.

He followed the sound of voices, careful not to give away his presence.

A woman stood there—*the* woman. She wore a sleek navy suit with a skirt that stopped just above the knee. She embodied the perfect mix of professionalism and sexiness. The flash of bare long legs brought back memories. He could see her only from behind right now but that angle looked really good to him.

Just as he remembered.

Her brown hair reached past her shoulders and ended in a gentle curl. Where it used to be darker, it now had light brown highlights. Strands shifted over her shoulder as she bent down to show the man standing next to her—almost on top of her—something in a file.

Not that the other man was paying attention to whatever she said. His gaze traveled over her. Spence couldn't exactly blame him, but nothing about that look was professional or appropriate. The lack of respect was not okay. As far as Spence was concerned, the other man was begging for a punch in the face.

As if he sensed his behavior was under a microscope, the man glanced up and turned. His eyebrows rose and he hesitated for a second before hitting Spence with a big flashy smile. "Good afternoon."

At the intrusion, Abby spun around. Her expression switched from surprised to flat-mouthed anger in the span of two seconds. "Spencer."

It was not exactly a loving welcome, but for a second he couldn't breathe. The air stammered in his lungs. Seeing her now hit him like a body blow. He had to fight off the urge to rub a hand over his stomach. Now, months later, the attraction still lingered…which ticked him off.

Her ultimate betrayal hadn't killed his interest in her, no matter how much he wanted it to.

If she was happy to see him, she sure hid it well. Frustration pounded off her and filled the room. She clearly wanted to be in control of the conversation and them seeing each other again. Unfortunately for her, so did he. And that started now.

Don't miss
REUNION WITH BENEFITS by HelenKay Dimon,
part of her JAMESON HEIRS series!

Available June 2018 wherever
Harlequin® Desire books and ebooks are sold.

www.Harlequin.com

Want to give in to temptation with
steamy tales of irresistible desire?

Check out **Harlequin® Presents®**,
Harlequin® Desire and
Harlequin® Kimani™ Romance books!

New books available every month!

CONNECT WITH US AT:

Harlequin.com/Community

 Facebook.com/HarlequinBooks

 Twitter.com/HarlequinBooks

 Instagram.com/HarlequinBooks

 Pinterest.com/HarlequinBooks

ReaderService.com

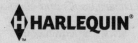

**ROMANCE WHEN
YOU NEED IT**

PGENRE2017